The Siberia Path

Book I: The Demon's Curse

BY

ABIGAIL C. HILL

Cleveland, OH

AChill Publishing LLC

2025

COVER DESIGN
BY SHENTEZZU

AChill Publishing, LLC
PO Box 31150
Independence, OH 44131

ISBN: 979-8-89619-771-3 (e format)
IBSN: 979-8-89619-774-4 (print)

For my brother, Matthew
my biggest fan.

10-31-2025

TO Nancy,

Thank you so much! I hope
you enjoy!

abigail Dahill

♡

Table of Contents

CHAPTER ONE

Demonic Discovery

Rain poured down onto the roof of the house. Thunder boomed, lightning slashed across the dark night sky, striking down a few trees along the way towards the small, red-roofed house on Yorkshed Avenue. Inside the little house, Alyson Siberia yelped at the sound of thunder and hid behind an old-looking couch. Watching his younger sister jump behind the couch, Claymore stood up from his spot on the floor and strolled over to the lumpy couch. Making sure that Ally couldn't see him, he got on his knees and knocked on the floor in front of the large piece of furniture.

"It's alright, the thunder stopped Ally," The boy said in his most soothing voice, then chuckled. "I thought you said you don't get scared of anything. Seems that's not true."

"I don't!" Ally immediately ran out from behind the couch and faced her brother. "When will mom and Elliot be home? It's been forever since she called that she was on the way."

"It's only been five minutes, silly. Mom and Elliot should be home any second now," Clay sighed deeply, glancing out the window for any sign of the rest of his family. Growing up without a father and the fact that his mother worked all the time resulted in Clay having more responsibilities than most kids his age. "You can start eating dinner if you're hungry, I already made everything. It's just chicken nuggets and fries today."

"Oh yeah, I forgot you can make food. I hope that mom teaches me to cook when I'm ten too!"

The little girl squealed, running into the dining room and pulling her chair out. Clay pushed it in for her as she started to eat her chicken nuggets. Each table setting had a glass of milk with a plate of fries and nuggets on it.

"In exactly two years tomorrow, you'll be ten. But that's not for a while. You still have time before you're old enough. Speaking of old, are you excited to become eight tomorrow?"

Ally grinned from ear to ear, her mouth full of nuggets. "Of course! Elliot's excited too! I asked him this morning about it before he left with mom. And I'm not gonna be that old, you know!"

"You'll be eight, that's old. I remember when you were born Al." teased Clay. "Also, don't talk with your mouth full, you know mom wouldn't be happy". Clay pulled out his own chair and sat down, nibbling on the ends of his fries. The front door creaked open, and two pairs of footsteps entered, closing the door behind them.

"Alyson! Claymore! We're home!" their mother, Cora announced from the hallway.

Elliot, who was Ally's twin brother, sped into view, hopping into his chair next to Ally and smiling at his siblings, his espresso brown eyes sparkling. "Ooh, chicken nuggets! I love these! Thanks Clay!"

"No problem. How was your doctor's visit?" Clay asked Elliot, taking a sip of milk from his glass.

"It wasn't as scary as I thought it would be! I didn't even need to get a shot. And after that, we said hi to the white puppy next door!"

"The doctor said that he should relax and take things easy for another day," their mother explained, walking into the dining

room. *"And about that dog. I don't think the owners will let her inside. I was thinking about taking the dog in here, they clearly won't miss her."*

Cora didn't sit down at the table to join her children. She took one look at them and headed to the living room window, where she stood in front of it, watching the storm progress outside.

Clay set down his glass and stared at his mother. "Is something wrong, mom? Did you not want the dinner I made?"

"Oh sweetie, that's not the problem. I'll sit down in a minute, don't worry."

"Then what is the problem?"

Cora froze, still watching the storm outside. Her hands were shaking. "It's nothing dear, just eat your dinner. You wouldn't want it to get cold."

"If you say so," Clay muttered, turning back to his food, a million thoughts buzzing in his head.

"Clay! Are you listening? Hello?"

Clay blinked, temporarily forgetting where he was. He didn't immediately recognize the pale empty walls that surrounded him, or the plain brown bed he was laying on.

The city of Cleveland roared loudly with the sound of cars outside his window. Then it all came back to him. The incident on the twin's birthday, nearly seven years ago, being brought to the orphanage with his little sister Ally, and Elliot and mom... He couldn't bear to think about it.

A girl with long snowy white hair and big oval blue eyes was sitting next to him with an annoyed look on her face. Her name was Lyly, another sixteen-year-old at the orphanage besides himself. Well, he assumed that she was sixteen. He never asked before. Lyly was tan, wore a tattered and faded oversized red hoodie, a gray skirt, black leggings, and dirty white tennis shoes with little lines on the ends, making it look like animal paws. Her hood, as always, was up, her hair in pigtails, a few strands in the front hanging out from under the hood. A crossbody bag was laying on the bed near Clay's foot, various random items rested inside, mostly pretty pencils and bandages. Her bag was white in the shape of a heart with white little angel wings on either side of it. She also wore a crystal blue necklace that Clay thought was cool.

"Yeah, sorry. I zoned out, didn't I?" Clay groaned, his messy caramel brown hair getting in his face again, a red streak in the mix of his hair, which he blew off his face so he could see. He knew his hair was a mess, but he honestly didn't care. He'd grown to like it looking messy after having it like that for years. The red streak was probably his favorite part about his hair. However, he'd never once put dye in his hair. He had the streak for as long as he could remember.

"Mhm, that's alright though. I do talk a lot, so I don't blame you," Lyly shrugged. "I said that the headmistress should let Ally live in my room so she's not alone all the time! You know, so maybe she'll be nicer to others."

"I don't know. I mean, I think that's a great idea but, um, have you noticed that Ally doesn't seem to like you very much?" Clay asked slowly, becoming very interested with the red streak in his hair, which had made its way in front of his face again. He blew on it gently and it bounced up and down on his face.

"I know, but maybe she'll grow to like me more if we were roomies. She'd learn that I just want to help her,"

"What do you want to help her with exactly?"

"Come off it Clay! Seriously, do you not pay attention to what I'm saying? I'd help her become a better person! She's really mean!"

"I wouldn't call it mean. Grumpy? Sure, but not mean."

"She calls me names all the time! That's mean!" Lyly pointed out, reaching forward and grabbing her bag. The contents nearly spilled out, but she caught them just in time.

"She does do that a lot, now that I think about it. I've seen her mouthing off to Headmistress Sherry a lot too,"

"I've never seen her do that, but that does sound like something she'd do!"

"I guess you're right. Do you know what's for dinner today? I'm starving." Clay asked, his stomach growling angrily.

"Burgers? Something like that? I'm not sure. We should be allowed to eat now, let's go see for ourselves!"

Lyly jumped off the bed, putting her bag back onto her shoulder. She ran to the door in Clay's room and stood there expectedly. Claymore nodded and slowly got up, making his way over to Lyly. She reminded him of a puppy sometimes. The way that her eyes lit up whenever she saw him, and the way that she acted around people. Calling her just an extrovert was an understatement. Lyly was the queen of making friends with almost any type of person, no matter who it was.

"Can I ask you a question?" Clay asked, herding Lyly out of his room, closing the door behind them.

"Sure! What is it?" Lyly raised an eyebrow at him, skipping down the hallway towards the smell of burgers as Clay walked alongside her.

"Do you think that we'll ever get adopted? I mean, me and Ally have been here for a good portion of our lives."

Lyly froze. "I'm not really sure. I'd hope so! You two are really nice! Well, at least you are!"

Clay hesitated. "I mean, deep down Ally is nice. She has her moments."

"I'd like to believe that. Maybe she just has trouble expressing it," Lyly sighed deeply.

When they got to the dining hall, the smell of burgers smacked Clay in the face. It wasn't a good smell though. It smelled like someone had tried to make a burger with tree bark instead of a patty. The room was full of tables with white tablecloths that went down all the way to the floor. Across the room was a medium-size door with a brass door handle that he assumed led to the outside world, but nobody ever went towards the door. The headmistress told them to never open it, or they'd get into huge trouble. And besides, the door looked locked so not an option even if they were thinking of getting rebellious.

When Clay and Lyly got to the dining hall, Clay's younger sister Alyson was sitting by herself in a corner of the room on the floor, a half-eaten burger laying on the floor at her feet, her eyes looking around wildly, paranoid about something. Ally had Heterochromia, a condition that meant she was born with two different colored eyes. Clay always thought that Ally's eyes were beautiful, they reminded him of his mother's eyes. Their mother Cora had yellow eyes that sparkled in the sunlight and brought joy to whoever her gaze fell upon. Ally had one brown and one yellow eye. The yellow one looked identical to the ones Cora had. Ally was very pale unlike Clay, and her hair was a lovely ash brown that went to the middle of her back.

Clay tugged on Lyly's arm, gesturing to where Ally sat alone. Lyly spun around and locked eyes with him before running over to his trembling sister. Clay knelt and tilted Ally's chin up, looking into her broken mix-matched eyes, trying to figure out what was wrong. There were no injuries that he could see. It must be a mental thing then.

Ally's eyes didn't have any expression at all. They haven't been full of much emotion since the incident. It was difficult to tell what she was thinking. She tended to keep her emotions and feelings bottled up inside.

9

"What's wrong? Why is your food on the ground?" Clay asked, letting go of Ally's chin after checking her over again.

Ally sighed and mumbled something under her breath to Clay, but it was so quiet that he couldn't tell what she was saying.

"Ally, we can't help you if you don't tell us what's wrong!" Lyly pointed out, sitting down in front of the girl, looking her over.

"I don't like you, go away you idiot," Clay's sister whispered, wrapping her finger around her shoelace absentmindedly.

"Al, she's not an idiot. Come on, you don't have to tell her if you don't want to, but you can at least tell me, right?" Clay prompted her, trying to sound as comforting as he could.

"Ugh. I just dropped my burger. It's not that deep." Ally rolled her eyes at him.

"And that caused you to look all paranoid and freaked out?"

"No, I'm not that stupid. There's something else. Something that I don't want to say in front of Lyly because she's annoying and I hate her."

"Ally, that's incredibly rude. Why don't you just tell me? I'm just trying to look out for you, you're my little sister!"

"Fine...I saw a demon. A real one, like I've been telling you for years and now it's probably too late, and we're going to get kidnapped by one." Ally whisper-shouted, still in the earshot of Lyly.

Lyly wrinkled her nose and started to giggle.

"Ally, demons aren't real. Just because someone doesn't like you, it doesn't make them a demon!" she said slowly like she was talking to a little child.

"I'm not lying, Lyly! Gosh you're so stupid! One of the kids here had horns! I saw it with my own eyes!"

"Like I said Ally, demons aren't real. Please stop making things up."

"I'm not making this up! There was a group of kids with horns and spiky tails! I saw them today! Oh, and their eyes were red! That's not normal!"

"When was this?" Clay asked his sister, looking into her eyes. "This morning?"

Alyson nodded slowly; Lyly put her hands on her lap, watching Clay carefully.

"Are you sure it wasn't the lighting? It might have been playing tricks on you," he continued.

"No, it was dark this morning! There were no lights! I saw it though I swear!"

Clay cleared his throat, glancing from Lyly to Ally. "Lyly, can we talk privately for a moment? Ally, you stay here and try to calm down, okay? Can you do that for me?"

"Mhm…" Ally nodded once more and continued to play with her shoelace.

Claymore stood up and dragged Lyly to the nearest abandoned hallway. Clay had a strange feeling about what Ally said. Even though she had claimed the same thing many times before, this time it just felt different. He put his hand on Lyly's shoulder and took a deep breath.

"I don't think that Ally was making that up. I believe her." Clay told Lyly, who looked dumbfounded.

"Really Clay? Demons? She's told us this a million times, and now you suddenly believe her?" Lyly raised an eyebrow at him.

"Mhm. She was acting differently about it than usual. Normally she's throwing books in our faces with various supernatural creatures in it. Ally looked scared, like something was actually coming for her. So, yeah, I believe her."

"Clay, demons aren't real! There's no such thing! The headmistress has told her many times the same thing!"

"Maybe the headmistress was lying to cover up the truth. She seems very shady," Clay found himself saying, which confused Lyly even more.

"Are you bloody insane? Nobody is out to get you guys, especially not the headmistress!"

"I'm perfectly fine, I just have a feeling that Ally isn't making this up. Why are you so confident that my sister is lying about this?"

"Because it's mad behavior! I have to go. I'll talk to you later," Lyly huffed, slapping Clay's hand away from her shoulder and stomping away angrily.

"See you later then!" Clay shouted after her, but Lyly was already gone. He cursed under his breath and returned to his sister's side.

"Do you think I'm lying? Do you think I'm crazy?" Ally asked slowly. Ever since the incident that landed Clay and Ally into the orphanage, Alyson had been convinced that the supernatural existed, mostly demons. He usually didn't take her seriously, but it felt different this time.

"You're not going crazy," Clay reassured Ally, rubbing her shoulder and humming softly. "Lyly sure seems to not believe you. I'm not sure what that's about."

Ally tilted her head slightly and glanced around. "I think I know what's up with her."

"Well, what is it? I'm not going to think you're crazy, no matter what you say."

"She's a demon, Clay. Sent to keep us from the truth!"

"Why are you so sure that she's a-"

Ally covered his mouth quickly before he could finish, watching carefully as a group of kids walked by with food trays. As soon as the kids left, Ally removed her hand from her brother's mouth, looking around wildly.

"Why'd you cover my mouth?!"

"We can't talk about this here, not in public. Meet me outside my bedroom tonight around eight, that way nobody will overhear." Ally told him, standing up and pulling her brother to his feet before walking away down a hallway to the left towards the girl's rooms which is the opposite from where Clay had originally come from.

"Not creepy at all," Clay muttered to himself as he walked down the hallway on the right going back towards his room. He just didn't feel hungry anymore after everything that happened, probably just nerves.

Claymore continued to walk down the hallway, he felt like he should be focusing on everything around him, even though nobody was there. He told himself that he wasn't being paranoid but should follow his instincts. As he was thinking, he was trying to look at the situation logically. Demons weren't real. There's no way they could be. It would be all over the news if they were!

However, as he continued to think, the more afraid he started to feel about it all. If what Ally said was true, why would demons be hunting them? Is that why they were attacked so many years ago?

The thought left his mind racing as a group of kids turned the corner and started walking towards him. It was a group of four or five, talking quietly to each other but when Clay got within hearing distance, they all looked up at him and stopped talking until he was further away. As he watched the group go by, he froze. The children didn't have shadows, and they were directly in the lamp light. There was something odd about their eyes. They had an unfriendly sort of tone to them.

A chill went down his spine and he quickened his pace as he rounded a corner, ducking into his room and locking the door behind him. Something was definitely off about the kids in the orphanage, and now that he'd noticed it, he wouldn't ever be able to look at them the same again. He had to tell Alyson when they met up later.

"I can't believe she was actually right about this, after all these years of me dismissing it," Clay muttered to himself, walking over to his bed and laying down, but not before he closed the blinds and double-checked that the door was locked. A sturdy door was one thing, but a locked door was better.

Maybe if he closed his eyes and thought about the abnormal things that were happening, they would all just disappear. He could gaslight himself into thinking that everything was normal again. That sounded like a good idea to him, even though he hadn't been awake for very long. Calming his breathing, he slowly closed his eyes as he tried to go to sleep. It had only been five minutes when he was snapped back to reality by a loud banging at his door.

"Who's there? I'm trying to sleep!" He yawned, sitting up in bed.

"It's Lyly! Please open the door, Clay!"

Clay rolled his eyes and climbed out of bed, walking towards the door. "Go away, Lyly. I thought you were mad at me for sticking up for my sister?"

"Look, I'm sorry about that. It sounded completely mad; you know? Of course, I wasn't going to believe what she said. She sounded crazy!"

"She's not crazy! She's just scared! Don't talk about her like that, alright?!" Clay growled, hitting the door with two fists as hard as he could without breaking his hands. "Did you just come here to make fun of my sister?"

"No, I didn't mean it! Clay, I'm sorry…" Lyly whispered, sniffing. Was she crying?

Clay froze. He knew that Lyly could get emotional sometimes for the littlest of reasons; she acted very immature for her age in Clay's opinion. He usually didn't say anything to her about it. He adored her usual happy attitude.

"Fine, I'll let you in. Only because you're adorable and I can't stay mad at you," Clay grumbled, slowly opening the door for her, then walking back to his bed and sitting down. He was right, she had puffy eyes at the moment. "Oh, come here. I'm sorry for yelling at you."

Lyly walked over to him and hugged him tightly, knowing very well that Claymore wouldn't try to push her away. She had worn him down over the last few months about hugging. He didn't used to be a big hugger, but all her hard work had paid off.

"It's fine. I know you didn't mean it." Lyly mumbled into his shoulder, holding Clay close to her.

"I don't understand how you can be so upbeat." Clay said after a few minutes of silence between the two of them.

"Well, I kinda block out all the bad things in the world and try to focus on the nicer things, like eating popsicles!"

"What is up with you and popsicles? You act as if they are the best dessert, you have ever had. They aren't that great."

"I love them! We don't get them often here; it's like a fun treat!" Lyly pointed out, slowly letting go of Claymore and wiping her eyes one last time to make sure there wasn't anything on them anymore.

"Oh yeah, I see your point. Do you like the raspberry ones more, or cherry?" Clay wondered, watching Lyly's expression change to bitterness, a rare thing for her.

"Raspberry ones are yucky. They taste like medicine and cough drops."

"I'm sure they're not that bad-"

"They are! They're gross! That's why cherry ones are better! They taste like the thing they're supposed to taste like!"

"Fair enough. So, is there another reason you're here or did you just come here to apologize...?"

"Oh, that... I didn't see Ally go back to her room at all. I thought that's where she was supposed to be going and I couldn't find her."

Clay stood up quickly, his mind racing through every horrible possibility that came to his mind. Normally if this had happened, he wouldn't have been so worried. However, the kids from the hallway got him thinking; did they have something to do with the fact that Ally was missing?

"We need to find her. Now. I-I saw something in the hallway that I'm not really sure about."

"What do you mean? What did you see?"

"I think Ally was right about the kids here being demons. The kids I walked past on the way here, didn't have shadows. I know she didn't mention shadows, but that's still very suspicious!"

"Oh god, not this again."

"I'm telling you; Alyson was right! I don't know how I didn't notice it before!"

"I can't believe you, Clay. We've been telling her that she's wrong for years. And now you suddenly believe her? Make up your mind!"

"Well, I'm sorry that I'm human! I can change my mind if I want to!"

Lyly looked Clay up and down like she wanted to tell him something but couldn't.

"Alright, fine but back to my point, Ally is missing for god's sake! We should be trying to find her, not argue!"

Clay sighed deeply. "Yeah. I hope nothing bad has happened to her."

"She's probably fine, but I agree with the little one," a voice said from somewhere in the room. The voice sounded like three people were talking at once. "It's been so long since I've been awake! Do people still talk with their mouths?"

"Excuse me? Who are you?"

"Sorry?" Lyly looked confused. "What are you talking about?"

Clay looked around wildly. "You didn't hear that voice?"

"No… Are you feeling alright Clay? I think you should take a short nap; you're starting to worry me a bit. Don't worry about Ally, I'll go find her. When you wake up, she'll be right back here safe and sound!" Lyly smiled and got off the bed, walked to the door and closed it quietly behind her.

"Ally's attitude will get in the way." The voice whispered in his ear, sounding amused by Clay's utter confusion.

"Who are you? I'm not going crazy, am I?!" Clay continued to look around for the voice but found nobody.

"You're not going crazy, if anything I'm going crazy. But nope, you're totally fine. One hundred percent a sane living being." The voice laughed like this was the funniest thing ever.

"If that's true, then why can't I see you?"

"I'm in your head, silly Claymore." The voice responded. "Where else would I be?"

"That's a lie, I'm not dumb. Where are you in this room?"

"Like I said. I'm in your head. Enjoy your nap, I'll be watching you, Claymore."

The voice was silent after that. Clay laid there for a few minutes before falling into unconsciousness, not knowing what danger he put himself and his family in by answering the voice's call.

CHAPTER TWO

Her Suspicion Was True

Alyson tip-toed down the girl's hallway, where all the girls her age slept. As she walked, she was careful to not step on the glass shards that littered the halls. There was normally a lot around the orphanage for some unknown reason, and every day she tried hard not to step on them. One time, she accidently hit the wall with her elbow because she was so busy trying to get around a pile of shards.

She didn't want to disturb anybody as she walked, especially because of what she knew about this place. Ally watched from her hiding spot around the corner, Clay walking towards his dorm. She considered following him for safety but decided against it. He could defend himself if he needed to.

"Miss Siberia, what do you think you're doing?" a voice said behind Ally that made her jump.

"Um, I'm just using my imagination and being a secret spy, nothing to see here." Ally lied quickly, turning around to face her worst enemy, Headmistress Sherry.

"Mhm. Alyson, I know that you're up to something, so please refrain from doing anything that could get you in trouble."

"Pft-me up to something? Never in a million years!"

The headmistress sighed, shaking her head, making her long and layered silver hair blow around. Her hair was always perfect, and it annoyed the hell out of Ally. This woman looked like she was in her early twenties, not someone old enough to be a headmistress as far as she was concerned. Her cornflower blue eyes glared at Alyson with their usual disappointed stare. She had on a red pleated suspender skirt, with gray knit tights, and black Mary Janes. She had light cocoa skin, and she was a very serious woman, who sucked the joy out of any conversation with the mere mention of chores and other boring assignments. Around her neck was a necklace with a small brass key attached to it. Ally noticed that she kept fidgeting with the necklace, something that made Ally look at her with suspicion.

"Oh, poor child, you know how I don't like being lied to." The headmistress crossed her arms looking irritated.

"You don't like a lot of things," Ally snorted.

"Excuse me? That was very rude of you. You shouldn't talk that way to your elders."

Ally just rolled her eyes and pushed past the headmistress. She had more important things to deal with than with her.

"Who does she think she is, trying to yell at me for walking around." Ally muttered, putting her hands in the pockets of her mint green jacket.

"What in the devil do you think you're doing?" a familiar high-pitched voice squeaked in front of her. Ally looked up into the face of Lyly, her brother's closest friend, and a real pain in the butt. She was always on Ally's case about running off and panicked her brother each time she did. Ally hadn't told Lyly where she was going, which was why she was surprised to run into her. Lyly seemed to always be near her, something Ally found very annoying. She really hated clingy people like that cheerful bitch.

"I've been asked that already; I don't need you hissing down my back too."

"You know that I'm just trying to keep you safe, right?" Lyly asked quietly.

Ally scoffed "Please. The only thing I'm in danger from is you, demon."

"What? Did you just call me a demon? You can't be serious!"

"As serious as a heart attack, Lyly. If that is your real name. Doesn't sound like a demon-ish name to me though. Is it a fake name?"

"Are you mad? My name is actually Lyly, and I'm not a demon! Why would you think I am?"

"Because, as I said, I believe that you are pure evil. Stay away from me and my brother." Ally continued, glaring down at her since Lyly was only around four foot six, versus Ally being five foot four.

"Oh, come off it! I'm not a demon! I'm just trying to protect you! Why won't you listen to me?!" Lyly snapped, looking very cross.

"You're crazy! Get away from me!" Ally stepped back, feeling her eyes start to burn painfully. It felt like she hadn't blinked for a long time. She was probably just tired or something. She wasn't feeling great for some reason.

"Ally? Are you okay?" Lyly looked at her, tilting her head to the side in confusion. Ally probably looked pretty stupid.

"Shut up!" Ally snapped, covering her eyes with her hands. She wasn't bleeding from them, so why did they hurt so badly? Maybe it was an internal thing, or maybe she was just imagining it? It couldn't be that though, the pain felt too real. Lyly sounded very confused, maybe it was a tactic she was using so Ally didn't know what was happening. Then again, Ally didn't think Lyly was smart enough for something like that.

Loud and memorable footsteps told Ally that the headmistress was approaching behind them. Lyly walked forward towards the headmistress, sounding chipper.

"Evening Sherry! Lovely evening we're having, eh?" Lyly beamed up at the annoyed headmistress. The headmistress walked right past Lyly without a second glance and stood in front of Ally.

"Alyson Siberia." Her calm voice was enough to make Ally look up. There was no expression on her face at all.

"Yeah? What do you want?" Ally grimaced at her, the pain in her eyes were slowly fading away.

"What in the world are you doing?"

"I was covering my eyes. Anybody with decent vision could tell you that."

"I'm aware. But why were you doing that? That's weird, even for you."

"I poked myself in the eyes. They felt like they were burning because that's how that works. Idiot," Ally glared. "Any other questions or can I go about my evening now?"

"You better not be lying, or you'll get more chores to do," said the headmistress coldly, turning on her heels and walking away down the hall towards her office.

Lyly smiled at Ally and grabbed her by the wrist, pulling her the opposite direction of Sherry. Lyly looked accomplished as she steered Alyson towards Claymore's room.

Alyson struggled, dragging her feet on the ground walking slowly. Lyly just pulled her along like a limp rag doll. Good thing nobody was around to see it. That would have been embarrassing. As she thought that, some blonde-haired boy walked past her, snickering in her direction.

"Loser!" The boy cackled and kept walking.

"SCREW YOU!" Ally flipped off the boy, then turned to glare at Lyly, who stopped pulling her and let her go.

"WHAT ARE YOU DOING, LYLY?" She hissed.

"I'm trying to get you to Clay!" Lyly said simply, shrugging.

Ally shook her head. "There are better ways to do that! And I don't need to see him, I must go to the library!"

"That's not important right now! You have to see him! I have a bad feeling."

Ally paused, not sure of what to say. "Alright, what's going on with you? This isn't about earlier, is it?"

"No! I mean yes! I mean- I don't know! I just have a feeling something bad is going to happen! I can smell it!"

"You're not a dog; people don't smell bad feelings. You must be a demon."

"How many times do I have to tell you?! I'm not a demon!"

"That's what they all say. Then next thing, you'll be calling your little demon friends and trying to eat me and Clay."

"For the last time, I'm not a demon! We should get back to your brother, he's worried about you. And also, that's really gross!"

Ally just narrowed her eyes at Lyly and slowly nodded. Even though she didn't always show it, Ally cared about her brother Claymore more than anything in the entire world, even if she didn't like his best friend very much. Clay always claimed that he would protect Ally from whatever came their way, though sometimes it felt like Ally was the one keeping him safe.

Lyly smiled and skipped away, opening one of the doors on the left side of the hallway. Ally walked over to her, peeking into Clay's room.

He was asleep, or at least Ally thought he was. His caramel-brown hair was super messy, but not like Allys. He just looked like that because of the style. A red streak, much like Ally's, was combed to the right side of his head.

"Just like I said before! Ally's safe and sound!" Lyly beamed at Clay, who sat up slowly, rubbing his eyes.

"Hey, Al. Where'd you run off to? I was starting to worry."

Alyson just shrugged in response. "I was just walking around. Am I not allowed to do that?"

"I mean you can, just let me know before you do so I know you're safe. Lyly had me worried about you."

"Yeah, yeah yeah. I'm not a little girl, Clay. I can defend myself if I really was in danger," Ally muttered, glancing at Lyly, who looked like she wanted to say something but didn't.

"Anyway, I really need to talk to you. Now. Without Lyly in the room. Family business." She stared at him, with a serious look in her eyes.

Lyly smiled, and skipped to the door, leaving quickly and closing the door behind her. Wow, she took the hint for once.

Claymore patted the spot next to him on his bed, signaling for Ally to join him. She rolled her eyes and walked over to him, sitting on the edge of his bed, staring at the floor.

"What's wrong Al? Is this about earlier?" Clay asked. He sounded so awake and alert for a person who just woke up. Ally thought that was interesting, how he could wake up and immediately start doing chores or other various tasks, no matter how long or little he slept.

"Sort of. It's just been bugging me. And I don't want to wait any longer to talk about this."

"Alright, then tell me. Maybe I can help ease your mind about this." Clay ruffled Ally's hair gently.

"It's just, I know I'm right and Lyly won't shut up about me being wrong. She's totally a demon. There's no other explanation for it!"

"Maybe. Anything is possible, if you're truly correct about demons being here, that is."

"You do believe me, right? She didn't get in your head and change your mind?" Ally mumbled, looking up from the floor to look her brother in the eye.

"No, she didn't. I still believe you, you goof,"

"Hmph. Thank you. Anyways, this doesn't have to do with the whole demon thing, but I saw something interesting earlier."

"You did? What was it?"

"You know that door that we're not allowed to open? That one with the brass handle right outside of the cafeteria?"

"Oh, geez where are you going with this-"

"Sherry had the key to it around her neck! We could get out of this demon plagued orphanage and find somewhere else to live that's safer!"

"Ally, as much as I'd like to leave this place, we have nowhere to go, and we have no money. We kinda need that to get anything in the real world."

"We'll figure that out when we get there! Come on Clay, we can finally get out! We're not going to be adopted, that's never going to happen,"

"Now that's a bit harsh. I'd like to think that someone would want us one day."

"Both of us? Or just you? Because there's no way anybody's going to adopt me, you know that!"

Clay sighed and scooted closer to Ally, putting his hand on her shoulder. "If nobody adopts you, and I age out, I'll adopt you. Got that? I'm not going to leave you behind, not ever. You're all I have left."

"You'd do that?" Ally's eyes lit up a little.

"Of course! Did you assume I'd just leave you here all by yourself? I would never do that! You're my baby sister!"

"I'm not a baby, but I get your point." Ally elbowed Clay in the side gently.

Clay chuckled and grabbed the back of Ally's hood, flipping it up so it covered her eyes. Ally yelled at him and fell backwards on Clay's bed, struggling to pull the hood off her eyes. Clay continued to laugh at his sister as she struggled. He would pay for that.

"Oh, you think this is funny, huh?" Ally hissed at her older brother.

"Well, yeah. It's hilarious." He grinned and chuckled some more.

Ally sat up and pulled her hood down, turning to Clay slowly. His grin faded as he realized what was about to happen to him.

"Hey, we can talk about thi-"

But Ally didn't let him finish. She lunged at him and tackled him, knocking both of them to the ground with a loud bang. Clay was laying on his stomach and wheezing, with Ally's legs crisscrossed on his back and her arms crossed.

"I'm sorry!" Claymore laughed, not even bothering to try and get up. He knew that he'd just get punched if he tried.

"Sorry isn't enough. Now you must pay for your mockery." Ally said sarcastically, reaching forward to start messing up his hair.

"Nooo my hair looked so good before! I spent days, years on that!"

"Too bad. You shouldn't have laughed at me."

Clay rolled to the side, pushing Ally off his back. Ally flopped on the ground and groaned in pain, her face in the dirty carpet.

"I saw something that you might find interesting, on the way to my room earlier, by the way." Clay stated after a few moments of silence, causing Ally to sit up quickly, her hair covering her eyes.

"Huh?" Ally moved her hair out of her eyes and blinked. Was her brother serious? No way.

"Yeah, I saw some kids acting weird, and they didn't have shadows. I know that's not what you saw, but it's still strange, right?"

Ally stood up, and grabbed Clay's wrist, pulling him to his feet. She had read in one of her books recently about these sorts of symptoms, but she couldn't remember what it was exactly. She thought if she checked the books in her room, they might have something useful in them.

"Whoa there, what's wrong?" Clay yelped as he was pulled up.

"I think that I read something about that earlier in one of my books I got from the library."

"That would have been helpful to know before you dragged me up!"

"Sorry Clay-"

Clay sighed and gestured to the door. "Do you want to get the book? It might be helpful. You clearly know more about these things than I do."

"Yeah. I have them in my room, come with me. It's safer."

Clay nodded and walked to the door, opening it up for his sister. She rushed out the door, Clay followed close behind her. Even though she didn't look it, Ally was extremely excited to show her brother what she's been hyperfixating on for years. Now that he believed her after all the times that she had brought it up before.

Ally was so deep in thought that she didn't even notice that they had arrived at her room until Clay tapped her shoulder, snapping her back into reality.

"Alyson? We're here, you know." He chuckled.

Ally rolled her eyes at him. "I knew that. Definitely. Shut up."

She grabbed her door handle and yanked it open, literally shoving Claymore into her room, hurrying in and closing the door behind her.

"Alright, I have them hidden just in case Lyly gets nosy. Wouldn't want her to tell the headmistress what I'm doing." Ally grumbled and laid down on the floor, looking underneath her bed.

She had a small pile of dusty old books, most of them were about various types of demons and other mythical creatures. She preferred reading about demons, as those were the most fascinating to her. Ally secretly thought it would be cool to be a demon based on what she's read about them. She could scare people away if they annoyed her. That would be amazing.

"Why do you think Lyly is a demon so much? I mean, I guess it's possible, but she's too nice to be a demon in my opinion." Clay said flatly, sitting down on the floor.

"It's not about personality. From what I've read, not all demons are essentially evil. They're just like normal people. They all act and behave differently. I think Lyly is a demon because of how close she is to you. She's constantly at your side, like she comes out of nowhere. That's not normal." Ally replied, pulling the books out from under her bed and wiping the dust off the covers.

"That actually makes sense. And here I thought you were going to have a silly reason. Guess I underestimated you sis."

"I'm not a little kid, as I've said. I don't always think that way. I'm fourteen, not five."

"It's crazy to think about. To me, I still see you as the adventurous little kid you used to be."

"Well, get used to this. I've changed. I thought that was obvious." Ally opened one of her books, the title being *Demons, One of The World's Most Terrifying Creatures.* She scanned through the pages, looking for anything that stuck out to her. This book was the first one she read at the orphanage. She had gotten in trouble for reading it at the time, as she was only eight, and she didn't sleep for two days after. Now, she could read it whenever she wanted. She just chose not to read it near the headmistress. Despite it being fun to argue with Headmistress Sherry, Ally preferred to be left alone about her reading habits especially now. Was it possible that even the headmistress could be a demon herself?

"I read something here about demons not having shadows. That would explain the kids you saw. I don't normally look to see if people have shadows, but I might need to start doing that. Have you ever looked to see if Lyly has one?" Ally continued, looking up from her book.

Clay shook his head.

"It's fine. She's probably not that far, so we can check next time she's near us. If she's not a demon, I'll be shocked. The signs are right there."

"What do we do if everyone here is a demon? I'm not sure about escaping this place."

"We would have to. This place makes me sick and if there's demons that want to hurt us here, I would rather leave. Besides, we've been here for too long. We know where that key is for the front door, we would just have to take it! Easy peasy!"

"How do you expect to take a key off the headmistress's neck? That's something she would definitely notice."

"We could distract her. Something along those lines. I'm annoying enough, so I can be bait."

"You're making it sound so simple,"

Clay sighed, and glanced at the book Ally was holding, reading the page she was on.

"What about that? Shadow Demons?" He pointed at a paragraph that Ally hadn't noticed at first.

Ally looked where he was pointing. There was a picture of an intimidating looking Shadow Demon in the middle of the page, with a description underneath and information on Shadow Demons.

"Shadow Demons, also known as Dark Demons, are creatures that were born from shadows. They can harness shadows and mold them into anything you could imagine, and more. Despite being referred to as sinister, these demons are one of the more friendly and peaceful types. Shadow Demons have gray skin, and pointy ears while in their normal demonic form. These demons don't have shadows, which makes them easier to spot in human society. Currently the strongest known Shadow Demon, Satoru, is the first Earth born demon to be a part of the Council of Demons," Ally read aloud.

"So, there's Shadow Demons living here according to this book. I wonder if there's any other kinds of demons around. What if there are Fire Demons? That would be cool." She continued, tapping the page she was on gently.

"I thought you were scared about demons trying to get us. What happened to that?" Clay asked nervously.

"Oh I am. But it's still really cool to know that I was right after all these years." Ally slammed her book shut, standing up abruptly. "We should try to get out. It's clearly not safe here."

"I agree with you, but I don't see any way we can without getting in danger."

"That's kinda the point. There's always risks when you try to change things. Remember what happened to mom?"

Clay stood up slowly. Alyson felt a little bad about bringing that up. She had almost forgotten how much that had hurt him. Sure, it hurt her too, but Claymore was really close to their mother. Ally was the free spirit that never sat still, and Elliot was the sensitive one that would follow Ally wherever she went, kind of like how Lyly does.

"Sorry. I just- never mind. We can go to her office and see if she left the key to the front door there. If we go through the kitchen, there's another door connected to her hallway, nobody will see us. Do you have everything you need before we leave? I think it would be best if we left now." Ally walked to her bedroom door and yanked a black bookbag off the back of the door.

"I mean; besides my coat, I have nothing. It's cold out, will you be fine with just a hoodie?"

"Yes, I will. It's warm enough for me. Don't worry about it."

Ally muttered, quickly shoving her books into the bag. "We should get some food from the kitchen and possibly a knife or something."

"What? Why do you need that?"

"In case someone tries to stop us. Clearly you know nothing about self-defense."

"And you do? Nobody's ever attacked us at this place!" Clay rubbed his temple.

"Well, it can't be that hard. If someone attacks me, I'll just stab them." Ally shrugged.

"No, I'll do that. You're not holding a knife. You could hurt yourself."

Ally grumbled and opened her bedroom door.

"Let's go before Lyly tries to join us."

And with that, she was off. Claymore followed close behind her. She didn't show it, but she was excited for the first time in a while. It was like an adventure. Their lives at risk, enemies at every turn. It was honestly thrilling. Nothing too exciting happened around the orphanage, so this was a change of pace.

Ally could remember her life before the orphanage very clearly. Her and her siblings were homeschooled, and they lived in the countryside. Their mother was a very sweet and patient woman. She never once yelled at Alyson when she'd do something bad. She would just sit her down and gently brush Ally's hair behind her ear. Then, of course, she'd proceed to tell Ally that she was in deep shit, but she did it nicely. Ally got grounded a ton.

It was impossible to regain that life. That dream had been crushed years ago, when their house was nearly torn apart, along with her mother, and twin brother. Ally's memories of the event faded with each passing day, each little detail swirling with another. But one thing she'd never forget was the person who tore her family apart. That image had been burned into her mind.

The figure was short with pitch black hair and one blood red eye. Most of its face was covered by the darkness. It looked like it had tar on it, but she couldn't tell for sure. It looked like it wore some form of suspenders, but it was difficult to make out in the darkness.

It also had something fuzzy on its shoulders. They had reminded her of angel wings, maybe really teared up ones, but wings, nonetheless. This being was no angel. Far from it.

She thought that she'd be next. That October 8th, she thought that would be her last day on Earth. No child should ever have to think about that.

Once they got out of the orphanage, Ally swore that she'd find her family's killer and show it what a mistake it truly made.

Ally and Clay rounded the corner, where the kitchen door was left wide open. It was near the end of the night, so there wouldn't be any cooks inside. Not like they actually cooked that food. If they did, they needed to go back to cooking school, because it tasted like shit.

"Is something wrong, Miss Siberia?" A voice said behind Ally.

Ally's eyes widened, both her and Clay stopped walking immediately. It was Headmistress Sherry in all her glory. She wasn't wearing the key to the front door around her neck, it had to be in her office.

"Now why would you say that?" Ally grumbled, staring at her shoes. She refused to meet her gaze.

"You don't leave your room often and when you do, you make a point to find and annoy me. Right now, you're doing neither but skulking around." The Headmistress stated. Dammit, she had a point. Why did this woman have to be so intelligent?

"I can change my habits!"

"People can do that, but you can't."

Ally rolled her eyes, grabbing her brother by the hand. They didn't have time for this nonsense. The kitchen was so close, and in turn, their freedom.

"Clay and I have somewhere to be, thank you." Ally said coldly, starting to continue walking.

"I would like a word, first." the headmistress said quickly.

Ally stopped, and so did Clay. They looked at each other, confused, and a little concerned. What could she possibly want? Did she somehow know their plans already? Was their chance at escaping the orphanage over?

CHAPTER THREE

Shadows and Knives

"Do I have to ask again, Claymore?" the headmistress raised an eyebrow at the siblings.

Clay turned around slowly, keeping Ally close to him.

"Alright, what is it?" Clay asked innocently.

"Clay! We don't have time!" Ally hissed in his ear.

The headmistress crossed her arms. "I want to speak with you alone, Claymore."

"What? Whatever you're going to say, you can say it in front of Ally."

"I prefer not. I don't want her temper to rise." she said calmly. This just made Ally even more angry. Clay could feel her anger rising, as she was squeezing his hand tightly.

"I think it's too late for that, ma'am." Clay laughed nervously.

"Hey buddy! How's it going?" A voice in the back of Clay's mind spoke. It was the same voice from earlier.

"Not now… I'm trying to talk to the headmistress. Can I please be crazy later?" Clay mumbled.

"Again, you're not crazy! You know what. I'll give you a little push in the right direction. Does that sound nice?"

"Claymore, who are you talking to?" Headmistress Sherry stepped closer to Clay, looking a bit worried. Ally tugged at his arm, trying to get them to keep going.

"Alright, get ready for a little thing I call, Demon Vision! Well, it's actually called True Sight but, my title sounds better. Anyways, ta da! Enjoy!"

Clay's vision began to blur. He didn't know if it had to do with the voice in his head, but regardless, it was not an enjoyable experience. When his vision returned, he found himself sitting up against a wall, the headmistress was kneeling in front of him looking concerned. Something was off though. As he glanced around, he noticed that everything had turned black and white. Nothing around him had any color. It was like something out of on old movie or television show.

Headmistress Sherry looked straight out of an old photograph like everything else in the room, except there were a few things different about her that sent chills down Clay's spine. On the top of her head were two shiny and sharp looking black horns about three inches tall. Next to her was a foot long tail with a half-heart shape on its end. Her features weren't human. She was a-

"D-demon." Clay stammered, hoping he didn't look as terrified as he felt. If he wasn't already sitting down, he probably would have fallen over from the shock. Alyson was sitting next to him tugging his shirt, trying to get him to snap out of it. She looked alarmed, but she didn't look like she was seeing the same thing he was.

Clay didn't waste any time to think any more. He got to his feet and pushed past the headmistress, grabbing Ally's wrist and pulling her away from danger. Ally was right, they had to get out of there and now.

"Claymore Siberia!" Headmistress Sherry yelled, running after them. Dang, she was faster than Clay thought she'd be.

"Get in the kitchen!" Ally pointed, steering Clay through the open doors in front of them.

Clay was running too fast. When they were about to pass under the doorframe, he tripped. He felt them both slipping, and he quickly grabbed his sister, holding her close to prevent her from getting hurt on the impact.

They slid across the kitchen floor, then slammed into the back wall. Clay's bones ached, he felt tired.

"Geez, learn to slow down next time!" Ally grumbled from his arms. She was alright, thank goodness.

Clay let Ally go as she glared at him. His vision had turned back to normal. All that crashing around must have fixed it somehow.

"Are you alright? Sorry Al, I didn't realize how fast I was going." Clay chuckled, lifting himself to his feet.

"Mhm. I'm fine. We should try and grab some food, before the headmistress-"

She didn't have time to finish her sentence. At that moment, the headmistress caught up with them and entered the kitchen.

"You kids are in a lot of trouble; I was talking to you." she stated flatly.

She didn't look like a demon anymore, but there was no questioning it. Headmistress Sherry was a demon, and she was trying to get them for reasons he didn't know.

Even though Ally didn't see the proof, she had believed Clay's words immediately and hadn't questioned them for a second. Something that he should have done for her years ago.

"Leave us alone! Go ruin somebody else's lives!" Ally yelled, looking around for a weapon. There was a long kitchen counter in front of them, various cooking supplies were resting there, such as pots, forks, and knives. Clay saw the weapons too and thought, "Oh goodness, Ally wasn't stupid enough to try something like that, was she?"

"I am the owner of this house, you have to listen to me," she walked right past Ally, shoving her to the side.

"Claymore, you are older, maybe you'll listen to reason."

She reached forward to grab Clay's arm.

Claymore didn't know what was going on, but he wasn't about to be carted away to some unknown location. If he disappeared, what would happen to Ally? He knew from experience that when she got scared or felt alone, she'd completely shut down and there wouldn't be anyone to help her.

Something happened when the headmistress went to grab him. The lights began to flicker throughout the entire kitchen, like someone was standing next to the light switch and flipping it on and off over and over again. Sherry didn't look too bothered by this, but it scared the heck out of Ally, who jumped onto the kitchen counter, grabbing one of the knives.

Clay glanced around nervously, not sure of what was happening. Did he cause the lights to do that or was someone trying to intervene? He tried to swallow his fear and took a step backwards, falling into someone's arms, something he hadn't expected.

"What the-" Clay mumbled.

The person holding him chuckled. There was something familiar about his voice. It sounded like three different boys were talking at once. One high pitched, one lower pitched, and one normal that had a hint of amusement all the time.

"It's a pleasure to finally meet you in person, if you don't count our little chats from earlier."

Clay, feeling super embarrassed and looked up at the boy. What did this boy look like? Was he real?

To his surprise the person looked around Clay's age. He had jet black hair that went a little past his shoulders, gray skin, and pointy ears. It looked like he had spent hours trying to make his hair look nice. However, there were a few spots that he missed. He had long gray horns on his head and a spiky tail. The boy had cherry red eyes that had a mischievous twinkle to them. He wore a vintage dark green sweater vest with a tie, a long-sleeved white t-shirt underneath, and gray jeans that seemed as if they were fresh out of the dryer, not a single wrinkle on them to be seen. Yes, he was very real.

"Satoru." Ally and Headmistress Sherry both said at once. Satoru... That was the name of the demon from Ally's demon book. The strongest Shadow Demon. But what was he doing here?

"You must let them leave. I know you're trying to keep them safe, but Nyx is going to find them one way or another." Satoru directed these comments to the Headmistress, and helped Clay onto his feet, giving him a friendly smile, before turning back to the headmistress.

"I understand that you're trying to help, and I'm glad that you are awake, but you have to listen to reason. They cannot leave this orphanage."

"I'm sorry about this, but they have to know the truth." Satoru clapped his hands. Something weird happened when he did that. The shadows on either side of him twisted and turned, their forms being molded for Satoru's desires. A pair of giant black shadow hands appeared at his sides.

"What the hell?!" Ally slid off the kitchen counter and stood by a stunned Clay's side.

Satoru made a fist with his hand, and the shadow hands mimicked his every movement. They spun around in the air, advancing towards the headmistress. She stepped to the side. Her hands glowing. The left shadow hand floated behind her, trying to pick her up by her hair, while the right tried to fan her away. Both plans were kind of working. She had to keep backing up to avoid the left hand, and she was being pushed right out the door by the right.

"Again, sorry Sherry!" Satoru yelled as Sherry was blown away down the hallway.

"Hey, so, my name is-"

"Satoru. We know." Clay said quickly. "What are you doing here?"

"Well, I want to start by saying and getting it out in the open that I am not a monster. I've been living in your head for almost seven years now. I was napping until recently." Satoru shrugged, keeping his eyes focused on the hallway Sherry was launched down.

"What's your angle, huh? You just appear, save us, and want to help us get out of this orphanage?" Ally glared at Satoru, holding the knife close to her.

"Well, yes. You basically summed it up!"

Ally rolled her eyes. "I don't know if I can trust you. Claymore?"

"I mean, he did just help us…" Clay whispered to Ally.

He was probably being very stupid. He figured that much but this guy looked like he was being truthful. Satoru may be a demon, but maybe they weren't all bad. Wasn't that what it said in Ally's book? Besides, they could use someone with magic or powers to help them in the real world.

"Ugh! I don't trust him! We literally just met him, and he claimed to be living in your head! That's so creepy!"

"Um, I hate to break up, whatever this is, but I can only hold her back for so long. So, you better get what you need and make it fast," Satoru chimed in. He looked like he was starting to get tired.

"Alright, Ally, get as much food as you can into that bag of yours. Then, we need to find the front door key from her office."

"Got it. But this conversation is far from over. We're talking about it later when we get the chance." Ally grumbled, and started opening cabinets, shoving whatever food she could find into her bag.

CHAPTER FOUR

Running Into Death

Alyson couldn't believe Clay. There was a demon living in his head, and he didn't find that suspicious? Sure, she still thought demons were pretty cool, but this was just crazy. She didn't trust anyone who just appeared out of thin air and then acted like they were there to help.

"Are you almost done?" Satoru called, yawning a couple times.

"Yes. Are you alright?" Clay stuck his head out from in the fridge. Ally told him that they couldn't take cold food, but he didn't listen to her as per usual.

"I'll be fine, it's just that using my powers takes a lot out of me." The demon yawned again.

"We don't have time for small talk! We have enough food in my bag, let's get that key, and get the hell out of here!" Ally barked at Clay, standing up and closing her bag, then putting it back on.

"Alright alright, geez-" Clay sighed.

Ally brushed her ash brown hair out of her eyes. The more they stayed and talked, the better chance Sherry had of coming back. Ally didn't want to stick around and find out what she was going to do to them.

"Do you want any help?" A familiar voice squeaked from behind Ally.

Ally turned around slowly, Lyly was standing right there, inches from her face, smiling up at Ally. It was like a jumpscare.

"What are you doing here?! Go away! We don't need your help!" Ally was beyond mad about Lyly's sudden appearance.

"You're traveling with a Humai? That's cool." Satoru glanced over at Lyly, then back at the hallway.

"Huh? Humai? Ally, do you know what that is?" Clay looked at Ally.

"No, I don't have a clue what that is. I am a demon expert, not whatever you're talking about." Ally shrugged.

"Humai is an animal creature. They're not well known and keep their true nature a secret until one is ready to believe. Can you not see the ears on her head?" Satoru mumbled.

"What ears-" Ally looked at Lyly again.

Lyly's appearance had changed, and Ally hadn't cared enough to notice. She could now see that Lyly had a pair of large, white, fuzzy dog-like ears on top of her head, and a white fuzzy tail. That was not there before, was it?

"I told you, I'm not a demon!" Lyly smiled and waved at Ally.

"So, you're an animal?" Clay raised an eyebrow, looking extremely confused.

"No! I'm a Humai, half animal, half human. There's a big difference!"

"...this is a lot to process in one day."

Ally nodded in agreement. "Alright, uh, cool, I guess. Lyly, why are you here?"

"I wanted to help you get the key and escape!" Lyly said quickly, her tail swishing from side to side.

"What? How do you know about that?"

"I overheard you! I hear everything that happens in this orphanage. That's the cool thing about being a Humai. I have amazing hearing!"

"Whatever. I don't want you coming with us." Ally rolled her eyes.

"Ally! She's coming with us!" Clay shot back.

"What? Why? Now you're trying to bring two people that weren't supposed to come in the first place?! Come on, it's supposed to just be me and you!"

"They could be helpful! Lyly is my friend, alright? I'm your older brother, so what I say goes. Got it?"

"Fine. But I am not happy about this!" Ally stomped her foot on the ground and turned around to exit the kitchen through the other door. She could see the headmistress's office clearly. The door had been left wide open. The key was sitting on her desk. Freedom was so close now.

Ally didn't care where they ended up going, if it was as far away from the orphanage as possible.

"Hurry, we have to get out of here, Sherry's coming…" Satoru yawned again, rocking back and forth. The shadow hands had disappeared. Shit.

"Satoru!" Clay ran to Satoru's side, and just in the nick of time. Satoru's eyes closed, and he was about to fall to the ground. Clay caught him before he could hit the ground.

"Shit, Lyly, make yourself useful and go grab that key! Right there!" Ally pointed at the key in the office.

"On it bestie!" Lyly grinned and ran out of the room.

"I am not your bestie…" Ally muttered, holding the knife tighter in her hand.

"We need to get out of here! Now!"

Right as Ally said that the ground shook. She froze. She couldn't move her body. Clay looked like he was having the same struggle as Ally, because she could hear him whispering to Satoru about not being able to move.

Ally felt herself being lifted off the ground ever so slightly, maybe a few inches at most. Her knife was starting to feel very heavy in her hand, but she didn't drop it. She couldn't move her limbs no matter how hard she tried.

"Alyson and Claymore Siberia. You have some nerve, throwing me out like yesterday's paper."

The disappointed voice of Headmistress Sherry spoke as she walked into the kitchen with glass floating around her entire body. She was holding a silver and white spear that was twice her size. Oh, and she had the demon features of horns and a tail that they all could see now. Great.

"You two are in trouble. I will only ask you this one last time. Go back to your rooms and we'll pretend this never happened." She mused.

"Like hell!" Ally yelled, glaring at her.

The headmistress frowned. "Alright, but let it be known that I gave you the option to pretend."

The shards of glass around the headmistress fell to the ground and began to spin around in a circle, spiraling upwards and taking the form of a fifteen-foot-tall cobra that took up most of the room. It had to stoop down so its head didn't go through the ceiling. Whenever it moved, it sounded like someone was shaking a glass chandelier. The snake rattled its tail, and tiny glass shards flew in random directions. A few seconds later they would come right back like paper clips flying towards a magnet. Its disturbingly glowing red eyes were staring right at Ally, and she felt her pulse quicken.

"You will be coming with me, both of you."

Ally felt her muscles loosen; she could move again. Perfect timing for it too. She landed back on the ground and stepped to the side as the snake lunged forward trying to bite her.

"Ally!" Clay cried, his limbs starting to work as well. He carried Satoru out of harm's way and ran out the door, entering the office.

"I'm coming! Hold on!" Ally threw her knife at the snake and then ran towards Clay.

She heard the snake hiss, but she didn't turn back. She just ran after her brother as fast as she could. She'd worry about the snake in a minute.

Ally ran into the hallway, just about to enter the office, when she heard a loud hissing right behind her again. She found herself being launched into the air by something large.

That snake had managed to smack her with its glassy tail. It hurt more than she thought it should have. She felt herself being lifted off the ground and sent flying into the back wall. That was going to leave a mark or five.

"Did you not hear me? You're not leaving this orphanage; it's for your own good!"

Ally couldn't see her, but she could hear her talking clear as day. She had flown at the wall face first. Ally could feel something hot and wet dripping down her face. Blood. It had managed to break Ally's nose with one singular swipe of its tail. Was it trying to kill her?

Ally slid down the wall, collapsing onto the floor. She regretted turning around to look at Sherry. At that moment the glass snake was trying to squeeze its way through the door frame. The headmistress was already through and trying to get the snake into the hall. The walls shook as the snake struggled. Headmistress attempted to pull the snake through. There was no way it could fit; it was too tall.

"Remus, please, just lose a couple thousand shards and you'll fit just fine. They could be getting away right now."

Ally stood up, wiping the blood coming out of her nose. She stared at the snake, failing to attack her, and decided to mess with it.

"So, is your snake going to do something or are you going to just stand there?" Ally chuckled.

"Oh, you'll see." She sighed deeply, pointing at Ally with her index finger. "Get the girl, now Remus!"

The snake hissed menacingly at Ally, it finally managed to get through the doorframe and lunged at her. Alyson ducked just before the snake would have bitten her head off. She wasn't sure of what to do, but she knew that she had to get to her brother somehow without getting killed by the glass snake.

She glanced into the office. She could see Clay, Satoru, and Lyly there. Lyly was holding the key to the front door looking worried. The headmistress didn't seem to notice them. She was too focused on Ally. Good. Ally could continue to be a distraction so the others could get out of the office without being noticed. While she distracted the headmistress, they could unlock the door then Ally could hurry after them and escape too.

"Hey, big snake!" Ally catcalled the glass snake, as it turned its huge head to face her.

"Alyson Luna Siberia! Don't talk to my snake." the headmistress sounded annoyed, with a hint of worry? Nah, impossible.

"I really hate snakes! Especially ones made of glass shards!" Ally continued, starting to walk backwards, staring down the cobra. Its hood popped out, which made a large gust of wind, nearly knocking Ally over. Its tongue hissing at Ally.

"Alyson! What on Earth do you think you're doing?!"

"Being really annoying!" Ally cackled, running away down the hallway. She saw the knife she threw earlier and picked it back up.

The headmistress's tail snapped and smacked the wall behind her. She sounded really mad now. That was good. Ally wanted her to stay away from her office.

"Remus, go get her! I'll deal with the others." Sherry commanded the snake.

Ally continued to laugh as she ran down the dark hallway. She could hear the snake slithering after her, but she didn't dare turn around. She knew if she did, she would not have the courage to continue her crazy plan.

"Come on then! Catch me if you can, Remus!" Ally rounded a corner, the snake hissed loudly, slithering after her, the glass scraping the floor, making a horrible scratching sound that echoed throughout the entire hallway.

"Claymore! You come back right this instant!"

"Never!" Clay's voice yelled from behind Ally.

She could hear two pairs of footsteps running towards her. Claymore and Lyly, most likely.

"Ally! We got the key!" Lyly squeaked, running next to Ally.

"How did you get around that snake?" Ally glanced over at Lyly.

"It didn't even see us! It seems to be focused on you!" Lyly said cheerfully, her tail wagging from side to side.

"Are you alright Ally?" Clay made it over to Ally, holding Satoru in his arms. The boy looked incredibly weak and tired which was weird. Ally had never read about demons being so weak. She read that they were strong creatures capable of mass destruction. Yet this one was barely conscious.

"Yeah, I'm just dandy," Ally said sarcastically. "What's wrong with Satoru?"

"I don't know! You're the demon expert, aren't you?" Clay narrowed his eyes at Ally.

"Hey! I've never actually met a demon before! Give me a break!"

With all the conversation and chit chat, Ally temporarily forgot about the glass snake, and the angry demon Headmistress

Sherry at their heels. Well, neither her, nor her snake forgot about the group. The snake slithered quickly in front of Ally, hissing menacingly at her. Ally glared at the snake and led the group around it quickly. She didn't want anyone to get hurt regardless of how she felt about Lyly.

However, as Ally was just about to pass by the snake it turned its head slightly. Ally froze where she stood, her espresso brown right eye and her yellow left eye staring right into the red glowing eyes of the serpent. Then without warning, it snapped at her. This time, Ally wasn't fast enough. Two of its short fangs were going right through her left hand, causing her to yell in pain, Claymore turned around to look at his sister. He looked scared.

Her entire body felt like it was shutting down. No, it can't end like this. She was so close to freedom. Why was the world doing this to her? Why couldn't she just have a damn break for once?! Her hand felt like it was on fire, she could feel the venom coursing through her veins, trying to kill her.

Ally collapsed on the ground, barely having enough energy left to lift her head up. Her vision was getting cloudy. She tried to concentrate and focus on one single thing in the room. Her brother was running back over to her, Lyly at his heels.

"Clay…" Ally croaked, watching as a window broke nearby, the glass shards forming into an octopus-like tentacle, grabbing Lyly around the waist and holding her five feet off the ground. Ally didn't have the strength to move at all. She could hear her brother running towards her, as her ear pressed against the floor where she collapsed.

"Ally!" Clay cried, sitting at her side where she could see him. He set Satoru down, who just leaned against Clay sleepily. Then Satoru's eyes became awake and alert upon noticing Ally.

Before she knew what was happening, she was lifted off her feet carefully and being held in someone's arms. It felt like nobody was holding her at all, but she knew someone had to be. Last time she checked, she couldn't float. Curious, she looked down and saw two large shadowy hands attached to nothing holding her gently.

"Oh, shadow hands. Nice…" Ally mumbled, looking around her, her vision swirled and was blurry. She looked at her brother and Satoru, but they were just two large blurs to her now.

Something shattered close by. It sounded like glass. Was the headmistress making another nightmare from glass, or did one of her creations blow up? Ally didn't have much time to think about it as she heard Lyly yelp, fall to the floor and then running over to her panting hard.

"Thank you…" The blur that was Lyly said, looking in the direction of Satoru.

"Mhm, don't mention it." Satoru yawned, sitting up.

"Oh my gosh, she's not going to make it without medical attention!" Lyly exclaimed, her ears going down.

"She's already too far gone, that snake's poison works quickly, faster than it should for any normal venomous snake." Satoru said sadly.

Wow, he was giving up on her. What a jerk! Ally's heart dropped. Was she going to die? No, she couldn't! She wouldn't die! Not like this!

"I…I'm not dying like this. Figure something out!" Ally screamed in pain.

"She's right, I won't just let her die! Come on, there must be something!" Clay muttered, sounding like he was seconds from crying. Ally wasn't going to leave her brother behind. No way.

"At least stop the bleeding!"

"How?"

"My bag has some bandages in there, near the bottom."

Ally could feel Clay slipping her bookbag off her shoulders. She could hear him opening the bag and going through its contents.

"How many books did you put in here Al?"

"Only the important ones."

"Alyson, there's half a library in here!" Clay exclaimed, rummaging through the bag.

Ally didn't feel good in the slightest. Her vision was beginning to go dark. She felt herself slipping away from reality, slowly dying right in front of her brother. Come on Ally, you can't die! You can't leave Claymore!

"Alyson, stay with us!" Satoru commanded. His voice sounded very authoritative, but not like the headmistress would sound when she tried to boss Ally around. This felt different. Then again, she was dying, so maybe that was it. She didn't want to let this demon boy down regardless. For half of her life, she read about demons. Now there was one right here. She couldn't die now, she had to know more.

"Ally! Stay awake please!" Lyly squeaked.

"No shit…Where did the headmistress and that snake go?" Ally mumbled.

"They're gone! I think Satoru scared them off!"

Ally groaned in pain. She felt sleepy. But she couldn't close her eyes. What if she died? What if she never woke up? Like hell, she wasn't dying in this orphanage, with her brother all upset like this. But as she tried to fight it, the harder it got.

"Oh, you poor thing. I have many people scheduled to die today, but you were not on my list." A voice said in Ally's ear. "You're so young, I hate having to collect the souls of children. It breaks my heart."

Ally mumbled; she didn't recognize that voice at all. It sounded comforting which worried her.

"Alyson Siberia? That is you, correct?" The voice continued.

"M…Mhm." Ally gasped in pain.

"I figured…I usually don't offer this sort of treatment but, would you be interested in making a deal?"

"Listen, I'm pretty sure…I'm about to die, I don't think I have time for deals."

"Oh, but I could fix that. We'll work out what your payment is later. Right now, all you have to do is agree and I'll not only save your life, but I'll take you and your friends somewhere safe."

"Fine, whatever! I agree!" Ally yelled with the last of her strength, and her vision went dark as she passed out.

CHAPTER FIVE

An Unexpected Reveal

Ally couldn't move. She couldn't see anything, and she didn't know where she was. Maybe she had just hallucinated a voice speaking to her and she had actually died in that orphanage.

"Ally! Can you hear me?"

Oh. Ally was hearing her brother. Yep, she definitely died, and he was calling for her from beyond the grave.

"Come on, wake up!" Clay's voice got louder in her ear. Now it was starting to get annoying.

"Alyson! Open your eyes!" This time, Clay was pretty much screaming in her ear. Enough was enough.

Ally opened her eyes. She was laying in the middle of a forest in a large portion of soft grass. Trees were scattered around her; some were in full bloom with various fruits. It looked beautiful and peaceful.

"Ally! Thank goodness you're alive!" Clay's cries could be heard next to Ally.

Alyson looked to her left. There was Claymore, sitting there and sobbing his heart out. Seeing him like that made her feel extremely guilty. He must have thought she was dead.

"Hey, Clay. I'm not dead, apparently." Ally whispered.

Clay pulled Ally close and hugged her, putting his head on her shoulder. He was trying to stop the tears from flowing but he wasn't doing a good job at it.

"I don't know what I would have done if you died!" Clay sniffed and patted her on the back gently.

"Probably exactly what you're doing right now…I'm sorry for worrying you."

"It's alright. I'm just glad you're alive. That bite looked bad. Luckily, Aurora fixed you right up!"

"Who?" Ally looked up at her brother, pulling out of the hug. She looked at her left hand. It was wrapped up in bandages where the snake had bit it earlier.

"Me." The same voice from earlier said in Ally's ear. Ally jumped and turned her head, looking behind her.

Standing there was a woman in a black cloak with a black hood pulled down. She had pale skin, mousy short brown hair and little freckles on her cheeks. Her ocean blue eyes stared intensely right into Alyson's soul. She was very tall, and her expression was difficult to read. Ally couldn't tell what this woman was thinking. The woman was holding a four-foot-tall scythe that looked like it could cut Ally into little pieces in an instant without any damage to the blade. Ally didn't feel like this was someone to mess with.

"I'm glad to see that you are in good health." Aurora said calmly, holding her scythe close.

"Where did you come from? Who are you?" Ally narrowed her eyes on the woman.

"I saved you. You were on the break of death. I gave you a choice to live or not, because you weren't scheduled to die so soon, Alyson Siberia." Aurora smiled.

"How do you know my name?" Ally grumbled.

"I know many things about you. I know that you're fourteen years old. You lost her mother and twin brother on your eighth birthday. You-"

"Shut up! Don't you dare act like you know my family!"

"Ally! Please!" Clay pleaded, trying to calm her down.

"I don't appreciate a stranger telling me about our family! The boldness of this woman!" Ally hissed, wanting to attack the woman.

When she looked back at Aurora, it was difficult to see her face. It was distorted and it gave Ally a headache to look at. She had no clue what that was about, but she kept trying to glare at the cloaked woman regardless of the pain.

"Don't strain yourself, Alyson. Now, let's talk about your payment. I already have an idea of what I want. The rest of your friends are waiting for us, my dear." Aurora turned on her heel and walked off through the trees.

"Hey! Get back here!" Ally yelled, standing up and running after the woman, dragging Clay behind her by his wrist. She wanted answers and Aurora was going to give them, no matter if she liked it or not.

Aurora slowed down as she heard them approaching. The woman stopped walking so Ally and Clay could catch up to her.

"You know, I was worried that you weren't going to follow. I'm glad I was wrong." Aurora chuckled, holding her scythe over her shoulder.

"Where are we going?" Ally called after Aurora, quickening her pace.

She sped up enough, so she was walking alongside Aurora. They were now walking on a neat little path. Ally didn't let go of Clay's wrist. She didn't trust this woman even if she supposedly saved Ally from a terrible fate.

"To my house, of course. I'd like to discuss your payment at my home, if that's alright with you. It's going to rain soon."

"Tsk, you're probably just saying that so you can kidnap us! No way."

"Ally, I think we can trust her. After all, she saved your life." Clay smiled nervously at Ally.

"Meh. Did you see her doing this or are you just taking her word for it?" Ally narrowed her eyes on her brother.

"Well, kind of? I saw her put the scythe on your wound and it closed."

"That's weird and it sounds made up."

"It's not. That's what happened!"

Aurora stopped walking, staring ahead of them. She didn't say anything, she just pointed her scythe in the direction of a house that appeared in front of them.

It was a large log cabin surrounded by pine trees, a little brick path leading from the driveway to the front door. Behind the house was a small lake. A bench was at the shoreline with fishing poles propped up against it. A wooden railing wrapped around the entire house, with hovering candles above the railings. Ally liked how their flames were changing colors softly. The flames were changing from blue to green, and then back to blue. A dozen black roses were in a neat flower bed in the front yard, a large dirt square resided off to the side. There was a small window next to the front door of the house. Right by the edge of the path that Ally, Aurora, and Clay were standing on, was a metal mailbox labeled, *The Thunderstones.*

"Thunderstones? That's a badass last name." Ally muttered under her breath as they approached the house.

Aurora walked in front of them towards the front door. She was reaching around in her pocket for something and cursing quietly.

"Why do I have so many keys…? What are these even for?"

"This is your house?" Clay asked, gently removing Ally's hand from his wrist.

Aurora nodded, not looking up from her mountain of keys. Ally could see the woman's face again. Aurora was wrinkling her nose.

"Ma'am, are you going to uh, open the door?" Ally rolled her eyes and crossed her arms, adjusting her book bag straps.

"I'm going to, in a moment, Alyson."

"It doesn't look like it."

Aurora put a key into the door lock and turned it. The door unlocked and she turned to face Clay and Ally.

"Your friends are in the living room." She told them, holding the door open with her scythe.

Clay and Ally hesitantly stepped inside the house.

Ally glanced around at the room as she walked in. There was a black leather couch and two matching chairs, blankets folded neatly over the backs of the chairs. A small fireplace stood in the corner of the room and a fire warmed the small home.

A kitchen could be seen in another room close by that looked like nobody had used it in years. Two staircases near the kitchen, one going downstairs and one going upstairs.

The living room was occupied by two familiar people. Lyly was curled up in a leather chair, sleeping. Satoru was lying on the floor, his eyes closed as well. They both looked tired and worn out.

Lyly's ears twitched, and she looked up at Clay and Ally. Her tail wagged with excitement, and she jumped off the chair.

"You're okay! Hooray!" Lyly smiled at the Siberia siblings.

Ally rolled her eyes at Lyly, not responding.

"It's always nice to see you in such a happy mood, Lyly." Claymore chuckled and pat Lyly on the head.

"Sit down, if you don't mind. We have much to discuss." Aurora told them all.

Clay sat down in one of the leather chairs and Lyly sat on the other one. Ally narrowed her eyes at Aurora and sat on the floor, sitting on her knees.

"That's not suspicious at all…" Ally muttered.

Aurora walked over to the couch and sat down, setting her scythe down by her feet. She looked calm and collected even though there were a bunch of random people in her house.

"The hard part is deciding where to begin. I'm not the best with these sorts of things." Aurora smiled nervously, fidgeting with her hands.

"Just get on with it already! Geez lady…"

"I was thinking of what to say, Alyson. But if you insist." Aurora took a deep breath. "I don't know how to say this lightly but you two are the children of Lucifer."

Ally froze, so did Claymore and Lyly. They all looked stunned. Ally and Clay were demons and children of Lucifer? The King of Demons? That was a lot to lay on them right out the gate.

"You're kidding, aren't you?" Clay chuckled nervously. Aurora just stared at Clay. She wasn't kidding. How in the world was that possible?

"How do you know that? And how do we know that you're not lying to scare us, huh?" Ally questioned, after a few more minutes of stunned silence.

"Your hair. Have you ever wondered why it's impossible to remove the red streaks?" Aurora asked calmly.

Come to think of it. Ally had wondered that her whole life. She guessed that Claymore thought about it before too, because he nodded in acceptance.

Ally had tried to cut that out of her hair before and it had always grown right back, like magic. Then again, in her books, it said nothing about Lucifer having children with magic hair.

Her mom hadn't spoken about their dad that much. There weren't any pictures of him to look at around the house. They had just assumed that he was a deadbeat dad that left to get milk and never came back.

Elliot always used to talk about how cool their red streaks were. All three of the siblings had them. Mom always told them that she didn't know why they had red streaks of hair. She told them that it made them even more special.

Ally had always thought that demons were cool. Hell, she was obsessed with learning as much as she could about them. She didn't ever think about being a demon herself. If that was actually true, it was sort of cool. Knowing that she's been learning about her own kind this whole time.

Alyson stared at Aurora coldly, picking at her nails absentmindedly. If this was how this lady started off conversations, dropping the most jaw dropping shit ever, what was next? She wanted to find out desperately.

"Okay? Is that all or are you going to spill the beans some more?"

"Give me a moment, please. I didn't expect you to react so calmly." Aurora blinked, her cloak blowing around gently even though there were no open windows to create a breeze. Maybe it just blew around like that on its own? Ally wouldn't be surprised if that was true at this point.

"At any rate, I'm sure you're wondering why you never saw your father or knew who he was. Correct?"

"Yes, I'd like to know where he's been or why he's never shown up to meet us before." Clay crossed his arms. Ally hadn't seen Clay behave so coldly in a long time.

"That's simple. If other demons and creatures knew that Lucifer had children, they'd come after you. That's why you two were placed in an orphanage. Enemies of your father would have harmed you both and used you as bargaining chips. It was for the best that he stayed as distant as possible," Aurora stated.

"Though, it appears that happened to your family before. One of my reapers visited your home, seven years ago. I was personally very busy, but I was told about the tragic event."

"Reapers?! Seriously!" Ally spat.

However, come to think about it, Aurora looked like a stereotypical reaper from her books, but Ally hadn't even considered that this woman was a reaper of sorts. She just assumed that Aurora was another type of demon.

"I'm quite literally this world's Death. So, no, I'm not kidding. After all, how else would I have rescued you from death?"

"I don't know! I'm not the one with magic here!"

"Actually, you do have magic and so does Claymore. Lucifer has powers of a Fire and a Shadow Demon. Meaning, you two should have both of those abilities. Whether you use them or not, they're there."

"Shadow Demon?! Like Satoru?" Claymore asked, looking down at the sleeping demon boy.

"Yes, like Satoru. He's the strongest Shadow Demon, not counting Lucifer, of course. I'm sure if you asked nicely, he'd gladly show you how to use those abilities later," Aurora put her hands on her lap, and nodded.

"Along with Shadow Demon powers, you also have Fire Demon powers as well. Though, those are harder to control. I'd advise trying to master shadow abilities first. They'll be easier to figure out, especially since you have the strongest Shadow Demon on your side."

Ally looked at Satoru. She decided that she wanted to impress this guy with her sick new demon powers. Ally always thought that demons were cool. Plus, Satoru seemed nice enough. He saved both hers and Claymore's lives after all.

"How about this? In the morning, Satoru and I can try and train you both and maybe your little friend here could help." Aurora gestured to Lyly, who was still sitting in the chair, zoned out. "That will be your payment not complaining about your training."

"Fine. That sounds fair. You did save my life after all. Thank you for that." Ally murmured to Aurora.

Ally snapped her fingers in Lyly's face, causing Lyly to blink a few times before focusing on the world around her again.

"Hi! Sorry, too many big words. Zoned out, heh." Lyly muttered, giving them all a friendly smile. Ally had almost forgotten that Lyly was even there.

Come to think of it, what was Lyly exactly? If she truly wasn't a demon, what was she? Some kind of humanoid dog?

Wait, she had said what she was before. A Humai? Oh yeah. Lyly did mention to her what that was before and at the time Ally didn't really care.

"How the hell is Lyly going to teach us how to use demon powers? She's not a demon." Ally pointed out, narrowing her eyes at the happy Humai girl.

"It's true that she's not a demon but that doesn't mean that she can't help you. She's still a magic creature like yourselves. Lyly probably knows more than you think," Aurora continued.

"I believe that the training will not only help you understand your powers better, but you'll grow as a person, and you'll be able to defend yourself against any monsters that cross your path."

"Monsters? Like, wendigo type creatures or-"

"Beings who want to capture you and hold you for ransom. You could call them monsters but there is one that I wanted to keep you two safe from…" Aurora's voice drifted off.

"What are you talking about lady? Tell us already!" Ally yelled, causing Lyly and Clay to jump in surprise.

"Ally! Don't do that without warning! If you don't mind." Lyly squeaked.

"Whatever, shut up Lyly." Ally rolled her eyes and glared at Aurora. "Care to explain some more?! Come on Aurora!"

Aurora sighed, looking a little worried. Ally didn't like it when adults seemed worried. If an adult was upset about something, it must be bad, right?

"The monster that I was referring to is one called Nyx. Have you ever heard of it?" Aurora asked.

"No, I've surely never heard of it." Claymore shook his head. Ally did the same, but Lyly nodded.

"Nyx is scary, I don't like hearing about it…" Lyly whispered, her ears going down.

"Well, they need to know what it is, Lyly. It's for their own good, and for their safety," Aurora reassured the dog girl, then turned back to Ally and Clay.

"Nyx is a combination of a few different creatures. It's a dog Humai, the same breed as Lyly, actually. That wouldn't be a problem if it was just that but, it happens to also be an angel."

"Now angels are real too?" Clay sighed.

"Well duh. If demons and weird dog people are real, why wouldn't angels and other creatures exist?" Ally fidgeted with her hoodie string.

"Your sister is correct. Rude, but correct," Aurora nodded in agreement.

"At any rate, the problem with it being an angel is that it's not a typical angel. A few centuries ago, something happened to it causing it to become violent. It turned into this monstrous goo creature that destroys anything that crosses its path. It can take control of corpses and any living thing and use them to carry out its cruel deeds."

"That sounds…pretty lame." Ally spat, after a few minutes of silence.

Aurora's gaze shifted to Ally. Aurora looked a mixture of anger and annoyance towards Ally.

"Ally, this is serious. You may not care now, but if you ever see it, I guarantee that it'll try to kill you. Stay away from Nyx, understand?"

"Understood! We'll both stay away! Right, Ally?" Clay stood up quickly, nudging Ally to do the same.

Ally grumbled and nodded. She didn't feel like arguing with her brother today. She was too exhausted after everything that happened. That and, she always felt guilty afterwards, when they did fight. She knew that Claymore felt the same way too.

"Oh dear, it's getting late. You should all be getting to bed. For the time being, you all can stay here. I already have your rooms prepared." Aurora stood up and picked up her scythe.

Lyly hopped off her seat, smiling. "Yay, bedtime!"

"Wait a second, how do you have rooms set up for us already? We've been talking this whole time!" Clay raised an eyebrow at Aurora.

"I set them up after I saved your sister from dying. I had some time in between that, and her waking up. Plus, I'm fast." She chuckled, and exited the living room, gesturing for them to follow her.

Lyly ran after Aurora, skipping happily. Clay walked after Aurora, but Ally didn't move. She was still trying to process everything that Aurora talked about in such little time. Nyx? What the hell kind of name was that? And why would this Nyx person try to attack them? Did it have something against Lucifer, aka their father? Speaking of that, Ally was still not over that. The King of Demons, her father? How?

As she was thinking, Ally felt herself moving. She blinked and looked around. Claymore was dragging her by her wrist, following Death and Lyly. Ally didn't bother to fight it; she was too tired to walk on her own anyways. It wasn't hurting her. Clay was usually very gentle when he'd drag her along unlike how Ally would drag him. She didn't mean to, but she always ended up hurting him. Aurora walked up the staircase to the second floor. It smelled like pine needles. Did she have some kind of scented candle up there? She hated those.

One by one, Aurora showed them their rooms. The rooms were basic log cabin styled with a twin bed in the middle, dresser on the left side against the wall and a mirror on the right side near the door. The only difference for the rooms were the colors of the beds and blankets. Lyly's were light blue, Claymore's were white, and Ally's were black.

Lyly and Claymore went to their rooms, leaving Aurora and Ally alone. Ally didn't have the energy to speak to Aurora, so she just ignored the woman and stepped into her new room.

"Get a good night's rest, Alyson. You'll start your training in the morning." Aurora smiled softly, closing Ally's door for her once she entered.

Ally heard Aurora's footsteps get softer, until she couldn't hear them anymore. She was on the verge of passing out from exhaustion. Ally barely managed to take her shoes off and tug herself into bed before she passed out.

Maybe this lady wasn't so bad after all.

CHAPTER SIX

Training and Picnics

Claymore woke to the smell of eggs, bacon, and burnt toast coming from downstairs. He sat up in bed and ruffled his hair. Things slowly came back into his mind from yesterday. Right. He was Lucifer's child, Lyly was a Humai, and one of the strongest demons in the world named Satoru was asleep on the floor in the living room. This was beginning to be too much for him. He didn't understand how Ally was so calm about everything. She was still her grumpy self when talking to Death about it all. Unless it was an act.

There was something on the end of Claymore's bed. It looked like clothes, but he couldn't be sure. He squinted his eyes as he wasn't fully awake yet. Everything was blurry.

Slowly, Clay got out of bed and stood in front of the pile of items on his bed. They were clothes. Aurora must have brought them. She really was fast when it came to taking care of him and the others. It felt nice after not having a mom for so long.

The clothes were a dark red flannel, a black t-shirt, black baggy pants, and hiking boots. There was even a small black brush so Clay could try and fix his hair if he wanted to.

He smiled a little to himself and quickly got changed into the new clothes. They fit him perfectly. He wondered if Aurora had gotten the others new clothes. Their old clothes were rather dirty after all.

Clay stood in front of his mirror trying to fix his hair with the brush. He didn't realize how knotted it was until he tried to brush it out. It hurt a lot. He remembered that his mom used to help him and his siblings with their hair. Oh, how he wished he was back in his old house with his two siblings and his mom and to be back to what it was before all this demon nonsense.

After about fifteen minutes, Claymore finally fixed his hair to the best of his abilities. He set the brush down on his bed and exited the room. He thought about going to wake up Ally, but he didn't want to for two reasons. One, he didn't know where her room was and two, Alyson was not a morning person. She'd throw the closest object at him if he tried to wake her up any time before noon.

Claymore descended the staircase, following the smell of breakfast to the kitchen. When he entered the kitchen, he was surprised to see that everyone was already there, even Ally was awake. Grumpy looking but awake.

Ally was sitting at the breakfast counter in the kitchen, angrily dipping burnt toast into the yellow bits of her poached eggs. Lyly was wandering around the kitchen and helping Aurora clean things up. Meanwhile Satoru was sipping something from a coffee cup, sitting on one of the other seats at the breakfast counter. Satoru and Lyly looked wide awake, unlike Ally.

It appeared that Clay was right in assuming that Aurora got the others new clothes too or at least, Lyly and Ally. Satoru looked the same.

Ally was now wearing a black sweater with some band name on it with some of the letters peeled off, gray jeans and new black doc martens.

Lyly had on a gray and white striped long-sleeved shirt with the sleeves rolled up, a baby blue skirt with matching light blue and white knee length socks. All the blue looked nice with her necklace that she always wore and of course to complete her outfit was her usual dirty white tennis shoes and her bag.

Claymore made his way to the last remaining seat at the breakfast counter, which was in between Ally and Satoru. Knowing Ally, he knew it wasn't wise to try and speak to her this early in the morning. So, he turned his seat to face Satoru instead. He wanted to ask Satoru something anyway and he needed his full attention.

"So um, did you sleep on the floor all night?" Clay asked, trying to make small talk as Aurora placed a plate of poached eggs, bacon, and toast in front of Clay.

Satoru took another sip from his coffee cup and turned slightly to look at Clay's soft brown eyes.

"Yeah, I was tired. Shadow Demons are powerful but also known for being physically weak if we use our powers too much. It's pretty pathetic if you ask me…"

"Is that why you were so tired after saving me and Ally at the orphanage?"

"Precisely! If I use my powers too much, I get tired and worn out but that's usually only if I'm making large shadow creatures that are bigger than myself. It's complicated." Satoru chuckled and set his coffee cup down, tracing the rim with his finger absentmindedly.

"Oh, that's interesting. Do you think that would happen to me, if I tried using Shadow Demon powers? Aurora said that I should be able to use them and that maybe you could help train me. Could you train me, and do you think that I would get as tired as you do using them?" Clay asked. He wasn't really a fan of fire. Shadow powers sounded easier to manage than flames. Plus, he had an excellent teacher right here.

"Maybe? I'm not sure. We don't usually have demons like you in Hell. But, if I had to guess, you probably would get tired, but nowhere near as tired as I get. I think it's because you are half human. That would be a question for the boss though. She's smart."

"The boss? You have a boss?" Clay looked over at Ally, hoping she might know what Satoru was talking about. Ally was still eating in silence, but she had turned slightly to eavesdrop.

"Yeah, Sherry's the boss of almost all other demons and reports directly to Lucifer." Satoru said, like that should be obvious.

"Sherry the headmistress is your boss? Why didn't you say that before?" Clay huffed. Sherry had literally tried to kill them, her pet snake almost killed his sister, and Satoru was just telling them this now?

"I thought I did! Besides, I haven't worked for her very long. I think it's been about five-ish, maybe six years now since I have." Satoru shrugged.

Clay froze. That was almost the exact number of years since the incident. There's no way, but is it possible that Satoru had something to do with it? He couldn't be the one who destroyed Ally and Clay's family could he? Clay saw the figure and from what he remembered it looked nothing like Satoru. Though, the years matched up…

Ally stood up slowly, staring at Satoru. Her eyes looked furious.

"It's been almost seven years. Not five, not six, seven!" Ally shouted, balling her fists and stepping towards Satoru.

"What are you talking about?" Satoru yelped in surprise as Ally grabbed him by his shirt collar, holding on tightly.

"I should have realized it sooner! You had something to do with the incident at our house, didn't you? That's why you are magically attached to my brother. Is that right?"

Aurora suddenly appeared behind Ally lifting her off the ground by the back of Ally's sweater. Alyson let go of Satoru, who jumped behind Claymore.

"Put me down you-" Ally growled, going off and saying some things that their mom would have scolded her deeply for.

"There's no need to fight. At least, not in my house. If you're going to get violent, save it for training if you don't mind."

Lyly was peeking out from behind Aurora, watching the interaction quietly. She looked disappointed in Ally's behavior. Clay had always wanted Ally to become a people person and get along with others, just like Lyly did. Though, Clay knew that would never happen. Ally hated everyone except for him.

"Anyways, if you're all done eating breakfast, we should start training right away." Aurora set Ally down. Ally flipped Aurora off, but Death didn't seem bothered by it. She didn't even react.

Ally stormed over to Satoru, ignoring Claymore's attempts to stop her. She poked Satoru in the eye and glared at him.

"I'm not done with you, Satoru."

"Ow! Watch the eyes!" Satoru whined.

Ally ignored him and continued going on her anti-Satoru rant. "I know you're involved somehow and when I find out, I going to kick your a-"

"Let's get to training!" Claymore exclaimed loudly, getting up from his seat and dusting himself off. He wished that he had time to eat, but he also didn't want Ally to beat up Satoru for something that might not even be true. Sure, the years lined up but that could just be a coincidence.

"We're going to be training outside. I already have everything set up for now." Aurora explained, exiting the house through the front door.

Claymore quickly followed Aurora with Satoru at his heels. Despite not knowing too much about Satoru, Claymore trusted him. He had a good feeling about Satoru. Besides, Ally's book said that Shadow Demons were friendly and peaceful. So far, Satoru was showing to be just that.

"Alright, what are we going to be doing? Like, what kind of training?" Clay asked, as they made it outside.

"I want to see if you can use your abilities without being taught how." Aurora said calmly.

Ally walked out of the house, still looking mad. "How are we supposed to use powers that we don't know how to use? That doesn't make any sense!"

"I know, I didn't think you could do it anyways. I mean, you're nowhere near strong enough to make a little flame." Aurora looked at the cloudless sky and sighed dramatically. Clearly, she was trying to trick them into trying. Clay saw through this, but Ally didn't.

"Hey! I could make these entire woods catch on fire if I wanted to! Watch this!" Ally growled and aimed her hand at Aurora.

Nothing happened, at least not for the first five minutes. Ally just stood there, cursing and waving her arms around, trying to make some flames. Eventually, she managed to make a small spark for a second before it blew out.

Aurora looked slightly impressed. "Fire abilities are harder to control, and master compared to shadow powers. Claymore, why don't you try to use flames? Maybe you're both stronger than I thought."

Claymore nodded and held his hand out, staring at it intently. He didn't know what he was supposed to be doing and he didn't think that it involved as much cursing as Ally did. So, he just tried to imagine a flame; the warmth and the power flames had in the palm of his hand. It didn't work. He was just standing there like an idiot, holding his hands out. How embarrassing.

"That's alright Claymore. Maybe fire powers aren't your strong suit? You're two different people, after all," Aurora's scythe appeared in her left hand.

"How about this? You train with Satoru, and I'll train with Ally. Does that sound alright?"

"Sounds good. Wait, what about Lyly?" Clay looked around, trying to pretend that he didn't just fail spectacularly. Did Lyly follow them outside? He was too focused on making sure Ally didn't start a fight to check if Lyly was with them.

"Oh, she's inside I believe. But, if she wants to help you train Claymore, she ca-"

"I wanna help!" Lyly squealed from inside the house. Within a few seconds, she was outside, ready to help. Even though she wasn't a demon, she wanted to help her friend. That was sweet of her.

"That was fast…" Aurora blinked, then waved Ally over to her. "Satoru, I'm putting my trust in you. I hope you know what you're doing."

"Yeah, I'll figure it out." Satoru smirked, pointing finger guns at Aurora.

Death walked off, Ally following suit. They walked to a small clearing that reminded Ally of a sand volleyball pit but without the volleyball net. So, just a pit of sand.

Claymore stood there and glanced over at Satoru. "So, how are we going to go about this?"

Satoru cracked his knuckles and walked a few feet away from Claymore. "I'm thinking, I can show you something that I can do and then you try to copy it. How does that sound, Claymore?"

"That sounds good! I think I can do that." Clay nodded, giving Satoru a friendly thumbs up.

The demon boy, Satoru, waved his hand from left to right. As he did that, Clay noticed the shadow of one of the trees peeled right off. The shadow swirled around in the air, looking like black smoke. The smoke twisted until it turned into a small bird made of pure shadows. It didn't even look real to Claymore.

"Hold your hand out, I think it wants to say hi." Satoru gestured to the bird and then to Clay.

Clay hesitatingly held out his right hand. The bird flew over to him and sat in the palm of his hand. It felt like nothing was there, but he could see the shadow of the bird.

"You can pet it if you want. It won't hurt you; I promise." Satoru smiled warmly at Clay.

He did want to pet the bird if it was even possible. He put his finger on the bird's head and petted it gently. It still felt like he was petting the air.

The bird nuzzled his finger making Claymore crack a small smile. He wanted to make something like this too. Satoru made it look so easy.

"Aw, that's adorable!" Lyly bounced up and down with excitement, running over to Claymore and petting the bird too.

"Can you do any magic like this Lyly?" Clay wondered aloud.

"Nope! I can just turn into a dog, that's about it. I have amazing hearing and my nose works really well." Lyly's ears twitched, and she giggled.

Satoru snapped his fingers and the bird disappeared. Lyly frowned and marched over to Satoru, holding her hands together.

"Can you make another bird? Please?" She blinked innocently.

"I'm not going to but I'm sure Claymore would love to try. Right Claymore?"

"Yeah, at least, I'm going to try to. Don't be surprised if it doesn't work. I don't think I'll be able to make anything." Clay sighed.

"Not with that attitude! You can do it Claymore!"

Clay sighed and mimicked the hand movement that Satoru had done before. Wait. Was it left to right? Or right to left? Did it matter?

Satoru and Lyly watched, as Clay waved his hand from right to left. Nothing happened.

"Is he doing it the right way?" Lyly asked, tilting her head to the right, her ears drooping down.

"He's gotta do it the other way, give him a second Lyly," Satoru said loudly. Clay felt his face flush with embarrassment. He waved his hand in the other direction, thinking in his mind about a small bird appearing.

"If you're having trouble, try closing your eyes! That's helpful, right?" Lyly shouted, turning to Satoru for reassurance. Satoru nodded.

Clay decided to try doing that. He closed his eyes. He imagined a small bird of shadows in the palm of his hand. When he was little, he used to watch birds outside with Elliot. He could sit there for hours watching birds in their backyard. Elliot loved to spend time with Claymore. Ally couldn't sit still that long, so she never joined.

He thought about those simpler times when his only worries were finishing his schoolwork before his mother came home from work or from running errands around town.

When Claymore opened his eyes, there was a bird made of shadows in his hands. It wasn't a small bird though. It was a raven.

He looked over at Satoru and Lyly to see their reactions. Lyly was hopping up and down for joy. She was always very supportive of whatever Clay did. Satoru wasn't saying anything, but he looked proud and that was enough for Clay.

"You did it! You made a bird! A bigger bird too!" Lyly squealed. Satoru clapped softly.

"Impressive! Now, make more birds." Satoru said flatly.

"What?" Clay blinked in surprise.

"You heard me. More birds!"

Was he serious? Claymore didn't think that he could make more shadow creatures. It was hard enough to make the raven!

"You can do it Clay!" Lyly cheered.

Clay sighed and focused again on his other hand. Another raven made of shadows appeared in his other hand. This continued over and over again until Clay had shadow birds covering his whole body. For shadows, they were heavy. They were perched on his arms, shoulders, and head.

"Am I done now? This is getting tiring, no offense Satoru." Claymore sighed. He couldn't move his arms. There were too many birds weighing him down.

"Alright, that's probably enough with the birds." Satoru waved his hand from right to left, the opposite way that Clay had made everything appear. One by one, the birds disappeared and shortly after Clay had feeling in his arms again.

"Thanks." Clay sighed and shook his arms a couple times.

"Do you want to try making shadow hands? They're better to use in combat." Satoru tilted his head slightly.

"Like the ones you used at the orphanage?"

"Yeah! They're a little tricky to make and you have to be able to focus on your own physical hands and the shadow ones at the same time. Think you could do that?"

"I won't know until I try, but sure." Clay mumbled.

Right as he was about to test it out, he felt a light tap on his shoulder from behind him. He spun around and came face to face with his sister.

"Al? What are you doing here? Aren't you supposed to be training with Aurora?" Clay said with a look of confusion on his face.

"Yeah well, we're taking a break." Ally huffed. She looked exhausted.

"And? How are you coming along with your abilities?"

"Just fine! I can make fire like nobody's business. I could set an entire house on fire if I really wanted to."

"Really now?" Satoru questioned, somehow standing behind Claymore. Clay didn't hear him approach at all.

"Yeah! Really!" Ally crossed her arms and stared at the Shadow Demon.

"Make a ball of fire that's larger than me then. Right now."

"Bet!"

Ally held out her hand staring at it intently. A small flame appeared in Ally's left hand. Impressive but not what Satoru had asked for.

"I can't do it with everyone watching!" Ally spat, after a few minutes of staring at the small flame.

"Are you sure that you can do it at all?" Lyly tilted her head, sounding doubtful.

"Tsk, of course I can! Shut up!"

"But-"

"Can it, Lyly!"

Before Ally could get the chance to strangle Lyly, Aurora walked over to them, the ends of her robe were on fire. She was coughing a little bit too. Clay was very concerned for whatever Ally did to Death.

"Your sister isn't that bad at using her fire abilities, but she needs a lot of practice. Also, she can't make fire that's bigger than her hand." Aurora stepped on the flames on her robe, putting them out.

"Oh, so Ally was lying about it? That's interesting." Satoru mused. Ally looked ready to punch Satoru. Claymore gave her a look of warning and she calmed down slightly.

"Before any fights break out, would you like to have lunch?" Aurora smiled, looking up at the sky.

The sun was in the middle of the sky already. How long had they been training for? Clay felt like his arms were going to fall off if he had to make one more shadow bird. He also skipped out on breakfast, which his stomach decided to remind him of, growling quietly.

"I have some sandwiches in the fridge. I'll go get them. We'll just eat outside, if that's alright with everyone."

"Yay, sandwiches!" Lyly giggled with glee.

Aurora turned on her heel and walked back inside the house. Satoru waved his hand and the shadows bended to his will, making a large blanket of shadows for them to sit on.

Ally glanced at the blanket, but she didn't sit down. Her leg was bouncing up and down. Ally didn't like to sit still. She always had to be moving. When she was younger, she didn't like to sit down and relax. Clay knew that was just a side effect of her ADHD, so he didn't question it.

"Ally, why don't you sit down with us?" Lyly waved to her, sitting down on the blanket.

"I'd rather stand, thanks..." Ally said sarcastically.

Clay sat down. If he hadn't sat down then, he probably would have fallen over from exhaustion.

"So, how did Aurora train you? I didn't see what was going on," Clay looked up at his sister. She was now pacing around the area.

"Oh, she had me try to make fire and I threw flames at her," Ally put her hands on her hips and tilted her head slightly. She had a very smug look on her face.

"That's really cool!" Lyly's tail wagged slightly. Ally stopped pacing to stare at her.

"I can't tell if you're trying to be annoying on purpose or not."

Clay was tempted to kick Ally. He knew that she was normally rude to others but he felt like she was at war with Lyly except it was one sided and Lyly was completely unaware of it. Lyly was usually nice to everyone even if they didn't seem to deserve it. Not that Ally didn't deserve kindness. Just that his little sister could be a jerk to others.

"Let's change the subject! Favorite color?" Satoru chimed in quickly.

"Blue!" Lyly squealed.

"Black- hey, you're tricking me into giving you information!" Ally marched over to Satoru and glared at him.

"What am I going to do with that-" Satoru sounded very confused.

"I don't know! Just… Ugh!"

At that moment, Aurora came back with the sandwiches. Perfect timing. Ally sounded ready to fight Satoru and Lyly and Claymore didn't want to have to pull her away from the others. He was not in the mood to deal with that.

"They're peanut butter and there's some ham ones in there as well. Enjoy!" Aurora set a tray of sandwiches down in the middle of the blanket along with four bottles of water.

Lyly took a peanut butter sandwich happily and thanked Aurora.

Satoru picked up a ham sandwich with his tail, keeping his hands on his lap. He was being very careful to not get any crumbs on himself. Clay had a feeling that if he got one crumb on himself, he'd freak out.

Claymore grabbed a ham sandwich as well and glanced at his sister. She should get something to eat even if she wasn't going to sit down with everyone else.

"Ally, do you want a sandwich too?" Clay offered.

Ally stared at the sandwich plate for a moment, before walking over and kneeling. She looked at everyone, then grabbed a peanut butter sandwich, and stuffed the entire thing into her mouth at once.

"I didn't mean- chew your food!" Clay sighed and shook his head. He really didn't want Ally to choke while trying to eat her food.

"I have to go to work. I'll be back in the evening. While I'm gone, you can explore the grounds if you want. It should be safe," Aurora announced, preparing to leave again.

Before she left, Claymore thought of something he'd be wanting to know for a while. He just didn't know when the right time was.

"You collect the souls of the dead, right? Since you're Death?" Clay blurted out.

"Why yes, that's what I do. Why do you ask?" Aurora turned to face Claymore.

Ally stared at Claymore. He knew that she knew what was going through his head. She didn't try to stop him. Ally wanted to know as well.

"I don't think we mentioned it but on October seventh, which was Ally's eight birthday, someone broke into our house and attacked us. Nobody told us what happened to our mother and brother. So, I hope you know where I'm going with this, ma'am."

Satoru's tail dropped his sandwich on the shadow blanket in surprise. Lyly had stopped eating her own food as well.

Aurora took a moment to think about her response. She closed her eyes, tapping her finger on her chin. After a few seconds that seemed like minutes, she opened her eyes and stared at Claymore, looking deadly serious.

"I never got their souls."

CHAPTER SEVEN

Face to Face

It had been a few weeks since their first training session. Claymore and Alyson had improved a lot. Clay was able to create smaller shadow creatures without feeling like he was going to pass out. He was able to make tiny hands similar to Satoru's.

Alyson's temper hadn't changed which was good in this situation because it helped her to use her abilities more. She refused to learn shadow powers. She just wanted to use the fire ones because in her words "they're cooler".

Speaking of Ally, her birthday had passed. They didn't have any sort of celebration as she had told Clay in advance that she didn't want anything special. Clay understood. Ally felt this way every year since the incident.

Claymore did wonder if what Aurora said was true that she hadn't collected his mother and brother's souls. He wondered what happened to them. Clay was sure that he saw his mother and little brother die, unless Aurora misspoke or lied? He hadn't brought the subject up since that day.

It was a calm fall evening. Clay and Satoru were sitting in the living room, drinking hot chocolate and chatting. Ally was who knows where, and Lyly was laying on the floor. Aurora was working again, so they had a lot of time to themselves.

"I'm glad that you're progressing so quickly with your powers! You're a real natural, Claymore!" Satoru smiled sweetly at Clay.

"You think so?"

"Yeah! Course I do!"

Lyly sniffed the air and sat up. Claymore looked up and sure enough, there was smoke in the air.

"I got this under control!" Ally shrieked from upstairs. They could all hear loud stomping and a thud. Was Ally trying to put out a fire? Maybe? It sounded like Ally was trying to beat out the flames. Gosh, Clay hoped that she was. He didn't want her to burn the cabin down.

"Are you sure that you don't want any help?" Clay called upstairs.

"No! I can handle a little fire!"

"She's going to burn this house to the ground. This is a log cabin you know…" Lyly muttered, her ears going down.

"I heard that!" Ally yelled.

Clay heard some more banging from upstairs. What was Ally doing now? He half expected the house to fall apart any second.

"I haven't burnt the house down yet and we've been living here for weeks!"

There was more banging on the stairs as Ally came tumbling down the staircase right into the kitchen.

"The fire's out!" Ally blurted, laying on the floor of the kitchen like this was normal. At this point, that was normal for Ally and Clay wasn't sure if that was a good thing or not.

"How many fires have you started this week? Four? No, five, right?" Satoru smirked, sipping his hot chocolate.

"Four. The first one wasn't even my fault." Ally snapped, staring at the ceiling.

Claymore chuckled and looked out the window. It was beautiful outside. He could feel the fall breeze coming through the windows. It felt nice that they could just relax here without worrying too much about getting to the dining hall on time and what not. Aurora's company and this set up was much better than life at the orphanage. Aurora would make meals for the five of them and chat at the table. She listened to whatever they said and had meaningful conversations. Aurora acted like a mother figure of sorts. Clay wished that it could stay like this. It was nice to feel appreciated but sadly, things couldn't stay happy forever.

The front door suddenly opened, and Aurora rushed inside slamming the door behind her aggressively. She was clutching her scythe in her hands so tight that her knuckles were turning white, and her eyes were open wide. That was not normal for Aurora.

"Aurora? Is everything okay?" Clay glanced over at her, getting up from his seat. Usually, Aurora looked calm. What was the matter?

"Nyx. It's…going to…attack on Halloween." Aurora panted dropping her scythe onto the ground. It made a loud clatter causing Lyly to run over to them to see what was wrong.

"Nyx?! It's going to attack?" Lyly's ears went up, and she spun around nervously.

Aurora nodded quickly.

Clay could hear Ally getting up and running towards them too. He knew it was her as Satoru walked more gracefully than Ally.

Sure enough, Ally marched over to them and got up in Aurora's face poking her in between the eyes.

"Alright what the hell is going on? Why would you know that information? Huh? Are you working for Nyx?" Ally growled at Aurora.

Death glared at Ally and pushed her away gently. Aurora wasn't messing around. She was scary when she was serious. Claymore hoped that he didn't see that face when he died someday.

"When I was out collecting souls, that creature was nearby. It attacked the person that I was there for. He was terrified but he told me that Nyx was talking about killing your father at his Halloween Gala. It seems that Nyx wants to erase your whole bloodline." Aurora muttered; her tone was deadly serious.

It was silent for a few minutes as Aurora's words played over and over in Claymore's mind. Nyx was going to kill their father? The same one that walked out on them. Should he feel

117

worried for his father or not care? He wasn't sure what to feel and he had so many questions. Everything was falling apart in his brain at that moment.

What were they supposed to do about Nyx? Aurora said to stay away from that creature. Also, they weren't that strong to begin with so fighting Nyx was out of the question.

"Fear not, for I have a solution..." Aurora crossed her arms and looked at Claymore, then Ally.

"Since you two are Lucifer's children, you might be able to convince him to get ready for war."

"How are we supposed to do that? I don't understand." Clay shook his head.

"Just, talk to him at his Gala. All demons are invited so you won't have any trouble getting inside. At least I don't think you'll have issues." Aurora picked up her scythe from the ground.

"But tomorrow's Halloween! We don't have enough time! We don't even know how to get into Hell!"

"It's okay, I'll teleport all of us there. It won't be too difficult."

"Hey! If you can go to Hell, why don't you warn Lucifer? Why do we have to do your dirty work?" Ally sneered.

Aurora sighed like this should be obvious. "I already tried talking to him once I found out Nyx was going to attack but your father is stubborn, he doesn't listen to anyone."

"Then um, how are we supposed to convince him?" Clay raised an eyebrow at Aurora.

"You're his children. That has to mean something. He's not a monster," Aurora shrugged, spinning her scythe. "Well then, gather your things and follow along. We should get going." and then she walked out the door again.

Clay nodded and turned to look at the others. Lyly was trembling from head to toe, Satoru just sighed and stretched his arms, and Ally wasn't even there. Where did she go?

"I'm ready." Ally whispered from behind Clay causing him to jump slightly and then he turned around to face his little sister.

She had her bookbag on which held her various books on demons. Her interest in demons would be very helpful especially since they were going to Hell, the home of demons.

She looked determined and a bit excited. Ally was most likely realizing the same thing that Clay did moments ago.

"You're gonna need my demon skills. I know more about demons than you!" Ally smirked, her eyes sparkling a little. Clay

119

missed seeing her look so happy even though the whole situation was a bit odd.

"Yeah, I guess you're right. You seem really excited for this. Aren't you nervous about the whole Nyx thing though?" Clay rubbed the back of his head.

Ally shook her head. "Hell no. I get to talk to demons. I'm not worrying about Nyx until it's time to mention it to Lucifer."

Clay was impressed that she wasn't nervous unless she was lying to him to save face which was very possible. He didn't question her further.

"Come on, hurry up and get outside! I want to get going already!" Ally pushed past Claymore and ran after Aurora.

Claymore stumbled backwards but he caught himself before he could fall and get hurt.

Lyly hopped over to Clay and smiled nervously at him. "You sound nervous... Are you going to be, okay?"

Clay nodded. "Mhm. The sooner we get this over with the better. What about you? You look a bit nervous too."

"Hell sounds scary, I heard that some of the demons eat people that enter Hell, that shouldn't be there! I'm not a demon; I don't belong there!" Lyly's ears went down.

"There's only one demon that eats people and she's probably busy. You'll be fine." Satoru interrupted walking around Clay and Lyly, standing in the doorway. Clay could hear Ally screaming about stubbing her toe outside.

"But that's still one demon! What if we run into it? What about the other demons? I don't wanna be eaten!" Lyly sniffed.

Clay pat Lyly on the head gently, trying to calm her down. "It's gonna be alright, you're not going to get eaten."

He didn't know if he was lying to her or not. Clay didn't ask Ally many questions about demons in the past. He definitely didn't ask if demons ate Humai or not.

"Yay... Thank you Clay!" Lyly smiled at him and skipped out the front door after Aurora and Ally.

Clay went to follow them, but Satoru put his hand on Clay's shoulder, causing Clay to pause and glance behind him.

"Hey uh, Claymore? Can I ask you a favor?" Satoru whispered quietly.

"Oh yeah, sure," Clay nodded in response.

"So, you know how I was living in your head and how I jumped out to save you and Ally at the orphanage?"

"Mhm, I remember that."

"Well, I wanted to ask if I could hide in your head again just until we get to the Gala. I'm not ready to face the other demons yet, heh."

Clay paused. Satoru did train him even though Clay was terrible at using shadow powers and besides, it wouldn't hurt, would it? It was just a being in his head again.

"Yeah, you can hide in my head." Clay agreed.

The second that he said yes, Satoru melted into the shadows. Clay felt a shiver go down his spine. Did that mean that Satoru was back in his head? Probably.

"Clay, come on. It's time to go!" Aurora called from outside.

"I'm on my way!" Clay hurried outside to join the group.

Aurora was standing in the sand area of the yard; a circle was drawn in the sand around her. Lyly was trying to build a sandcastle, and Ally was cursing under her breath, standing nearby and grumbling.

"What did-" Clay began, but Aurora cut him off before he could finish.

"She stubbed her toe. She's fine," Aurora spun her scythe in the air and sighed.

"Is everyone ready to go? Do you have everything you need?"

Lyly looked up from her sandcastle and nodded, smiling a little. Clay was glad that she was in better spirits than before.

Ally took her bookbag off and started going through it quickly, nodding to herself. At one point, she paused and looked up slowly.

"I think I left my knife in the house-" Ally said slowly.

"Oh, for crying out loud Alyson..." Aurora sounded so disappointed.

"Alyson, go get your knife. Claymore, if you don't mind, please go with her so she doesn't get distracted."

Claymore nodded even though he was just in the house two seconds ago.

"Come on Al, let's get your knife and get going." Clay walked back towards the house, Ally following behind him.

"I thought I packed it! This is so stupid!" Ally rolled her eyes, putting her bag back on properly.

"Well. You're the one that forgot it. The only person you can be mad at, is yourself,"

"I'm two seconds away from punching you Clay,"

"Gotcha." Clay chuckled, opening the door to the house.

He didn't know why, but something felt off even though he had just been in the house moments ago. It felt different. Maybe it was because he was going to be leaving it so soon. That couldn't be it, they would come back here after they tell their father about Nyx, right? Clay didn't see himself living in a castle with a father that he had never spoken to before. That would be kind of awkward.

Ally walked ahead of him as they walked into the kitchen. Her knife was sitting on the counter. At least they didn't need to go that far into the house to find it.

"Got it. Let's go Clay." Ally picked up the knife and studied it for a moment.

Clay couldn't shake that feeling away. Something was wrong. What was it?

"Ally, do you feel like something's off, right now?" Clay asked, hoping she'd have an answer, but Ally shook her head looking up from her blade.

"No. Not really. Why?" Ally sounded a bit worried now.

"Just humor me please. I feel like I'm being watched."

Ally looked at Clay like he was nuts. He had to admit, he did sound a bit crazy, but he knew his gut was right. He just had to figure out what was wrong. Maybe if he walked around the feeling would go away or he'd discover the source of the disturbance.

Clay walked out of the kitchen and crept into the living room. He could hear Ally's footsteps behind him. He investigated the living room expecting nothing but leather furniture.

Something or someone was sitting on the couch staring at him and his sister. The creature was short, maybe a little taller than Lyly. It had long pitch-black hair that reached the floor. Its hair was a mess. It didn't look alive. Clay could see the faint outline of suspenders and a tie on the creature, underneath a mountain of some black goo substance. The only thing with any color on this creature was one blood red eye and some blood covering its hair. There was a hole where its right eye should have been. Its face was so distorted.

It was difficult to make out anything under the goo besides its red eye. There were small dog-like ears on its head and black wings that stretched across the entire couch. Though the most disturbing thing about this creature was the goo. It wasn't just on it. It was covering the whole couch, the wall behind the couch, and the area around it.

Its arms looked like they had been twisted and broken, then covered with the corrupted substance. This thing's proportions made no logical sense, anything in this bad of condition shouldn't be alive let alone sitting there peacefully without making a sound.

It didn't speak for a while. Nobody did. Clay was staring at the creature in horror, his hand trembling. What was that thing? Why was it here? What did it want?

Then he realized who or what it was. It was the creature that Aurora warned them about and the whole reason that they were about to leave. Nyx. The corrupted angel.

Clay slowly turned his head to look at Ally. She was on the floor on her knees, her eyes fixed on the creature in terror. Tears were streaming down her cheeks, and she was shaking uncontrollably. Her knife was still in her hand, held tightly.

Nyx continued to stare at them tilting its head from right to left. The only sounds in the room were the dripping of goo onto the floor and Ally's sniffling. Clay felt like he was frozen in place.

He remembered that thing. The night of the incident. It was there. Clay saw it.

Clay's head was pounding like someone was aggressively hitting it repeatedly. He wished it would stop.

"Claymore! Get outside! Move! Please!" Satoru's voice shouted at him in his mind. Oh yeah. He was in Clay's head again. That's what that pain was from. Satoru was trying to snap Clay out of it.

Clay blinked a few times and grabbed Ally's shoulders, shaking her. "Ally! We need to get out of here! Come on! Get up!"

Ally didn't say anything or move. Her eyes fixed on Nyx. Clay looked over at the goo creature again. It was moving.

Nyx hopped off the couch and slowly stumbled towards them, a trail of goo following its footsteps. Wherever the goo went, it stuck like glue and started spreading around the rest of the living room, like some kind of virus.

Nyx's head dropped down, frozen in place, staring at the floor. Was it trying to speak? Clay couldn't tell. Could it speak?

Clay kept shaking Ally, trying to get her to move. She wouldn't budge. He was heavily debating on picking her up and running but he didn't think he could move his legs either.

"Dammit! Clay, you need to move, now!" Satoru said in his mind. Clay couldn't move. The only thing he could do was shake Ally and try to snap her out of it.

A black gooey tentacle looking thing rose from the goo behind Nyx and grabbed Nyx's head tilting it upwards, so Nyx was staring at Clay and Ally again. Clay could make out the faint outline of a twisted smile where its mouth should have been.

Nyx laughed and the tentacle let go of its head. The tentacle snapped forward to try and grab at Clay and Ally.

Suddenly, Clay's legs seemed to be working on auto pilot as the tentacle reached towards them. He grabbed Ally lifting her onto his back and slid backwards, the goo tentacle inches from his face. Clay had a feeling that he shouldn't touch the goo. He didn't know why he felt that way.

The tentacle fell to the ground in front of him and melted into the floor. He told himself to run. Get outside to Aurora and Lyly and don't let Nyx take Ally away too.

Nyx stared at him, and more tentacles appeared. These ones picked up the furniture around Nyx and started throwing it at Claymore. He ran with Ally on his back as fast as he could to the door, nearly getting hit by the flying furniture. He whipped the front door open and made a run for it. His heart was pounding out of his chest. It was difficult to run while carrying someone and dodging furniture at the same time.

Aurora was standing outside with Lyly waiting for Clay and Ally to return. Clay hurried over to them scared to turn around. The looks on Lyly and Aurora's face said enough. Nyx was following him.

Death spun her scythe around glaring at the house as Clay ran over to them, taking a second to turn around. Nyx was stumbling towards him. The entire front of the house was covered with the goo substance. How did it spread that fast? Aurora did mention that it corrupts anything it touches, but still!

"It appears that I won't be joining you in Hell, after all," Aurora said softly, staring at Nyx, not taking her eyes off the creature.

"What?!" Clay exclaimed. She was going to leave them?

Lyly's ears went down, and she looked at Ally, who had managed to scare herself to sleep.

"I'll catch up, I promise. Just get to the castle and tell your father what's going to happen. I'll hold Nyx off for as long as I can."

Aurora tapped Lyly, Clay and Ally with her scythe, and they all disappeared. The last thing that Clay saw was Aurora walking towards Nyx, looking furious.

CHAPTER EIGHT

The Fire Demon

When Ally woke up, she wasn't at Aurora's house anymore. Also, her hand really hurt, and she wasn't touching the ground. What in the hell was going on?

Ally glanced down. She was holding her knife in her right hand. How did she manage to keep hold of her weapon while she was asleep? Damn, she really was a badass.

"Where are we…?" Lyly questioned. Ew. Lyly's voice was not the first thing Ally wanted to hear after waking up. She'd rather hear Sherry lecturing her or the sounds of cars beeping at each other aggressively during rush hour.

"Satoru says that we're in um, Infernoville? I don't know what that is…" Clay muttered.

"Huh? I don't know what that is either..." Ally muttered, looking at her surroundings. Her eyes were burning from the tears she shed earlier. She noticed that she was on Clay's back. Ally didn't remember that happening, but she was too distraught to question it further.

Ally would never admit it but at that moment when Nyx showed up at Aurora's house, she thought that it was the end. It felt almost exactly like the day of the incident. She and Clay stared at that angelic monster as it destroyed her family right in front of her. She tried to keep silent while she hid with Clay, despite all the tears flowing down her face.

This was just a repeat. Only, there was no hiding. She was fully exposed and vulnerable. Even though she knew how to create fire now, it's like all that training went out the window the second there was immediate danger. Ally felt ashamed. What if Clay hadn't moved in time? What if he died because of Ally's inability to fight back?

She could handle demons just fine, but that thing was her limit. Her nightmare on repeat for the past seven years. She despised sleeping because she was too scared to see that thing in her dreams.

Ally snapped out of her thoughts of misery and torment by her brother setting her down. She stood there feeling like a zombie as she clutched her knife in her right hand. Ally didn't even register where she was at first.

"Ally! Are you okay?" Lyly looked up at Ally, her ears were both down.

Ally didn't have the energy to be mean, so she nodded her head slowly looking around.

It looked like a typical busy city, like New York. It had skyscrapers, other tall buildings and even fast-food joints around except with a lack of taxis and more flames. A lot of the words on the buildings weren't in English, maybe Latin. She wasn't sure.

The air was red and smokey. The sky was difficult to make out. The smoke made it nearly impossible to see all the way up. They had to be in Hell. What other place would look like this? The entire city felt off, like everyone was holding their breath waiting for something bad to happen.

Some demons were wandering the streets chatting among themselves. Ally was surprised to see many different types of demons, not just shadow and fire ones. Ally didn't recognize most of them. Some had large horns and some had tails that were different shapes that Ally didn't know were possible.

"We're in Hell…" She muttered, the excitement wearing off as she breathed in the smoke and immediately started wheezing.

"I don't want to get eaten…" Lyly hid behind Ally, shivering. Ally had no clue what the hell she was talking about.

"You're not going to! It's fine Lyly! Besides, there's nobody going near us." Clay shook his head, looking around the area as well.

After a little while, they started walking down the street, Clay in the front. Satoru, from inside Clay's head, was providing him directions on where to go. Lyly was staying close to Ally, holding onto the back of Ally's bookbag as Ally put her knife away. Usually, Ally would have thrown Lyly into next week, but she understood where Lyly was coming from. If Ally didn't think demons were cool, she'd be scared to.

Slowly though, the other demons that were walking around took notice of the trio. Many stopped and stared at them. A few even bowed to Clay and Ally. She thought it was weird, and she didn't say anything to the demons that did that. Clay got all embarrassed each time and thanked them.

"Clay, where are we going?" Ally grumbled after a few more minutes of walking in circles.

Clay kept muttering to himself as they walked. There's no way they were lost. He had Satoru telling him where to go. Did Satoru forget where to go?

"Clay!" Ally walked ahead of Clay, standing in front of him. Lyly was still standing behind Ally, but she had let go of Ally's bag.

Claymore nearly ran right into her. He looked like he was zoned out. "Sorry, Satoru is getting confused or something."

While they stood there, a crowd of demons started to form whispering to each other. Ally's eye twitched in annoyance wishing they'd just leave.

"Do you people mind? I'm trying to have a conversation here!" Ally turned towards the crowd and glared at no one in particular.

"I didn't know he had children..." One of the demons muttered, completely ignoring everything Ally was saying.

"They're definitely his! They have the streak!" Another gasped, sounding excited.

"Oh, I see! They look just like him!" A third demon exclaimed.

Ally was two seconds away from setting all these demons on fire but before she could do that, the crowd started to part ways. A couple demons even ran away hiding in their apartments or various shops. Ally could hear the clicking of a pair of heels approaching, but she couldn't see where they came from. Someone in the crowd, maybe?

As the other demons parted ways, a figure emerged from the crowd from behind Claymore. Ally recognized this demon from her book almost immediately. Ally had to admit that this demon looked prettier in person. Ally was slightly intimidated by her too despite her always wanting to meet a Fire Demon.

The demon was about 6'5", with crimson red skin. Her skin has patches of a lighter red with a fire pattern on her wrist, triceps, and on her upper thighs. She had a pair of markings underneath her eyes, the same color as the fire pattern ones; only these were straight lines.

Ally could see that the Fire Demon's smiling teeth and claws were sharp and could probably tear her to bits if she wanted to. Her hair was made up of pure flames, dancing in the air on her head. Also on her head were a pair of matching horns that looked like they were made of fire as well. She had a long tail that was constantly swishing around, never staying in one place for too long.

The demon had two different eyes. Her left eye was Prussian blue but instead of having a matching eye, or even an eye at all in her right socket, there was a white shiny orb with flames bursting to life. The flames roared violently like they were trying to escape.

Her outfit was very similar to one that a circus ringmaster would wear. She wore a dark red tailcoat with the sleeves rolled up, a black corset over a white collared shirt underneath, black shorts, and dark red high boots. She carried a black and red comically large mallet in her left hand and was smiling wildly. And the name of this lovely demon? Only the strongest Fire Demon known as Scarlett or as she's usually called, Scar.

"Well, well! What's all the commotion about?" Scar asked cheerfully, spinning her comically large mallet around on the ground by the handle. She sounded like she was about to deliver a sale's pitch at a car dealership.

Clay turned around and stared at the demon. Ally could see that his hands were shaking slightly. Lyly was staying silent behind Ally shivering. Heck, even she was a little nervous.

Nobody answered. The crowd just stared at Scar and the scene that was unfolding.

Scar looked at the others, then at Clay, Lyly, and Ally. Scar's eye lit up with excitement and she floated towards them. Yup. Floated. She wasn't even touching the ground.

The head Fire Demon tilted her head taking notice of Ally. She must have looked upset or something because Scar raised an eyebrow at Alyson and floated right in front of her.

"You look like you've seen some dark stuff kid! Turn that frown upside down!" Scar giggled, spinning around in circles, hugging her mallet close to her.

One of the demons from the crowd stepped forward nervously. It looked like another Fire Demon. The demon looked at Scar like he wanted to say something.

"Um, Madam Scar?" The demon quivered.

Scar turned around slowly, smiling at the demon. Her fangs were out on full display. She hadn't stopped smiling since she showed up. Creepy…

"Well, you see, I-I mean, we think that you should spare these kids! Right guys?" The demon turned around to look at the rest of the crowd. Some of them nodded.

"Yeah! We think they're Lucifer's kids-"

Before the demon could finish his sentence, Scar jumped with excitement swinging her mallet around. She "accidentally" hit the demon who went flying off in the distance. The crowd looked horrified. Scar didn't say a word about it, like this was normal behavior for her or something. Or maybe, she truly didn't care that she just flung a fellow demon to his possible death.

"Luci's kids?! Oh wow, that's crazy! Didn't think he had a heart at all! Or good looks to make someone love him! Ha!" Scar threw her mallet into the crowd. A couple bonks told Ally that she injured more demons.

Claymore finally spoke after being in stunned silence for the past couple of minutes.

"Yeah. We're Lucifer's kids. Who are you?"

Scar narrowed her eye at him, floating around Clay, like she was looking for something.

"Have we met before? You seem, familiar,"

"N-no, I don't think so?"

"Hm, okay!" Scar stopped floating but instead of standing on the ground, she was standing on Clay's shoulder like some kind of acrobatic performer.

Clay stumbled slightly but Scar didn't move at all. She just hummed, her tail occasionally smacking Clay in the face. Lyly tugged on Ally's sleeve, still frightened.

"What now?" Ally grumbled and looked down at Lyly.

"She's going to eat me!" Lyly kept shaking Ally frantically.

"Huh- no she's not. What are you even talking about?"

Scar looked at Ally and held out her hand, flexing her claws dangerously.

"Actually, I am a bit hungry." Scar admitted, jumping off Clay's shoulder landing and standing on the ground behind Lyly.

Lyly shrieked and her form changed suddenly. No longer was she a human looking with animal ears but now she was an actual dog. A tiny purse dog in fact. Small, white, and very fluffy looking. She jumped into Ally's arms, trembling. Man, she really was afraid of getting eaten and Scar looked like she might try to do just that.

Ally wasn't going to throw a dog down like that. She didn't like Lyly, but she couldn't bully her when she was like this. It felt wrong, though it was difficult to hold a dog and a knife at the same time.

"Hey, back off. You're not eating my frie- I mean, my brother's friend. Okay? Now piss off!" Ally glared at Scar, who just laughed.

"Wow, you're very rude! Do you wanna know what I do to people that are rude to me?" Scar's smile got larger, her eye staring into Ally's soul. Ally felt a shiver go up her spine, but she tried her best to not look fazed by Scar's sudden switch up.

"Can't say that I do, and I don't care enough about you to find out." Ally put her knife away into her bookbag, so it would be easier to hold Lyly.

"Oh ho, you're really testing my patience kid!" Scar continued to stare at Ally with a serious expression. Her smile didn't falter for a second. She just kept smiling even wider.

"Scar! Leave them alone!" A voice said behind Ally. Satoru's voice. Guess who decided to show up, finally.

The Fire Demon stopped and looked behind Ally. Satoru was standing there alright with two large shadow fists at his sides, awaiting a fight. But a fight didn't start, quite the opposite happened. Scar flung herself at Satoru, nearly knocking the poor boy over in a hug. Her tail was swishing around faster than before, and she looked relieved. Satoru's shadow hands disappeared quickly.

"You're alive! I knew you couldn't have died that easily!" She cheered.

Satoru muttered something and patted Scar on the back before she let him go. He seemed a bit happier now.

"Nyx really tried to take me out. But I prevailed, as you can see, Scar." Satoru grinned and spun around.

Claymore looked at Satoru, then at Scar. "You know each other?"

Satoru nodded. "She's my co-worker. She might seem scary, but I promise she's not."

Lyly's ears twitched but she didn't say anything. She continued to stay in Ally's arms.

Ally narrowed her eyes at Scar, a thought coming into her mind. If Satoru and Scar worked together would Scar know if Satoru was involved in the incident? Better yet, what if Scar was there?

"Hey, Scar. I have a question for you." Ally announced a little too loud for Scar's liking.

The crowd, Clay, and Scar stared at her. Yeah, she shouted that loud. Whoops.

"Eh? Shoot, kid!" Scar grinned, spinning around in circles.

Clay's eyes widened slightly, and he shook his head repeatedly at Ally, but she ignored him. She wanted answers and she was going to get those answers the easy way or the hard way.

"Seven years ago, my house was attacked by Nyx. Do you know anything about that?" Ally growled.

Satoru slowly started walking away but Ally noticed quickly and glared at him. He stayed put after that.

Scar tilted her head in confusion and shrugged. "Can't say that I do! I was suspended when that incident happened. Though I did hear about it from Satoru! Ain't that right little buddy?"

Satoru looked like he wanted to disappear into thin air. He took a couple of deep breaths and tried to sound calm. It wasn't working.

"I have no clue what you're talking about!" His tail flicked around nervously.

Ally's gaze shifted back to Satoru. She knew he was involved. He might not have been the one who attacked first but he definitely knew something.

Scar blinked and stood in front of Ally, shielding Satoru.

"Hey now, let's not fight! Why don't you ask your dad about it? I'm sure he'd love to tell you!"

"Oh yeah. He'd be thrilled." Satoru said sarcastically.

Scar held her tail in her hand and spun it around. "I was just going up to the castle anyway! Can't be late for the Halloween party! Sherry would be mad if I was late again!"

Ally raised an eyebrow confused. "No, that's tomorrow. Today is the 30th,"

"It's Halloween, I think you're getting the dates mixed up!"

"I'm not! It's not Halloween yet! We have a whole other day!"

Satoru stepped out from behind Scar looking a tad nervous. Damn, Ally must have shaken him up. Cool.

"I forgot to mention, but time moves differently in Hell, and other parts of our world. No matter where you are, it's always one day ahead. So, it's technically Halloween down here."

"You're full of shit. Are you lying to piss me off? Because it's working!" Ally gritted her teeth. If she wasn't holding Lyly right now, she'd punch Satoru into next week.

"I'm not lying! You can ask anyone down here and they'll tell you the same thing," Satoru sighed.

"You probably told them to agree with you! Since you're so high and mighty down here!"

"Ally! That's ridiculous, I didn't do that!"

Clay stepped in between them putting his hands up. "Alright, that's enough! Ally, he knows more about this place than we do. I know you read your books, but he probably lives down here!"

"Don't take his side!" She stared at her brother in annoyance.

"Hey, guys! Stop doing whatever you're doing!" Scar floated around all of them, grabbing her mallet from a demon in the crowd, and swinging it around to get the kids attention. After that, she held her mallet close, letting the head of her mallet rest on her shoulder.

"You're hurting my head! Let's just go to the castle, I heard there's going to be little hotdogs!" Scar started floating away down a dirt path that seemed to lead towards a dark castle in the distance.

Clay, Satoru, and Ally looked at each other, nodded, and followed Scar begrudgingly. The crowd that was standing around them slowly shrunk and disappeared as there wasn't anything interesting happening any longer.

"Come along! It'll be an adventure! We can even play games! Like, whoever argues next, gets hit with my mallet! Doesn't that sound fun?"

Nobody replied. Lyly shivered in Ally's arms. Ally hesitantly pat Lyly's head. Damnit, and after all that talk about not wanting to be Lyly's friend. Oh well, as long as Lyly wasn't super annoying Ally could allow her to be her friend.

"I'm sorry about that, Claymore." Ally heard Satoru whisper to Clay.

Clay smiled softly. "It's alright. At least you apologized… Have you ever been to one of these Halloween parties at the castle before? What are they like?"

"They're just a fancy party for the residents of Hell to enjoy. Nothing out of the ordinary from your human parties."

"I haven't been to a party in years-"

"Really? That's a shame. I'll invite you to my birthday party in January! Then you can say that you've been to parties."

"That's nice of you! How old are you turning?"

"253!"

Ally paused, then smirked. "You're old."

Satoru shook his head. "Demons work differently than humans, Ally. I'm sure a demon expert such as yourself would have known that."

"Hey, my books didn't say anything about how old you are!" Ally snapped back as they continued to walk.

"That's fair… Well, demons are kids, or in my case, teens, until 254. That's like your eighteen, the age of adults for humans, right?"

"Uh huh. Your methods are weird."

"So are human ones, but I'm not complaining about them and making a big fuss."

Ally's face flushed with embarrassment, and she kept her head down. After a little while, she felt a tap on her shoulder. It was Scar.

"What do you want?" Ally rolled her eyes.

Scar smiled innocently. "Getting shown up by another demon. That must suck!"

"I don't need your input. Leave me alone."

"Ah ah ah! I'm not finished yet Ally! I want to make a deal with you!"

"Like I haven't heard that before. What do you want?"

The Fire Demon's white orb glimmered, and her smile widened slightly. "You call herself a demon expert, don't ya? Yet, you don't even have a demon to talk to. Not counting Satoru. You don't seem to like him very much."

Ally kicked some dirt while she walked, sighing. "Eh. He's alright, I guess. What are you getting at?"

"I could help you out with learning about other demons! I'm 10,000 years old after all! I've seen a lot of different types of demons come and go!"

That sounded perfect. Despite Scar herself being annoying, Ally really liked the concept of Fire Demons. That's partially why she wanted to learn how to use fire abilities before shadow ones. That and fire powers are cooler as far as she was concerned. Having a demon to tell her all the things that the books couldn't, could be useful.

"Really? What's the catch?" Ally looked down at Lyly, who was asleep in her arms.

"Oh. Nothing special. All I want…" Scar's tail snapped at the air, and she stopped walking. Ally did as well, staring dead ahead.

"…is to hijack your mind!" Scar clapped her hands together.

Ally froze. What was she talking about? Wasn't that how Satoru and Clay were? But she didn't want that! No knowledge was worth having someone in your mind. That sounded horrible.

From her experience with Satoru and Clay, Clay looked crazy when he was talking to Satoru when he was in Clay's mind, and it looked painful. Scar was not going to use Ally as a vessel!

Satoru and Clay stopped walking and stared at Scar in utter shock, and a little bit of horror.

"Hell no." Ally turned around to face Scar.

Scar stared at Ally for a minute not saying anything. Her teeth gleamed and she didn't move a muscle. Then, out of nowhere she attacked. She grabbed Ally by the shoulder, sinking her claws deep into her shoulder. Ally winced in pain and nearly dropped Lyly, who was somehow still asleep throughout the attack.

Satoru stared in horror at the scene before him. Clay started to run towards them with a couple of shadow hands reappearing at his side, ready to fight Scar but before she could do anything more to Ally. Scar waved her tail around and a ring of fire grew around Ally, Scar, and Lyly caging them in and keeping Satoru and Clay out.

"Ally!" Clay yelled, coughing behind the wall of fire and smoke.

Ally stared at Scar and kicked her a few times in the stomach causing Scar to let her go.

"Gah!" Scar yelped, stumbling backwards a little.

Ally backed up, trying to find an opening out of the fire. Apparently having fire powers didn't make her immune to the flames.

Lyly's ears twitched and she hopped out of Ally's arms landing on the ground. She stretched and turned back into her humanish form. Her eyes were watering, and she was covering her mouth with her hands.

"What's happening? Why is there so much fire?" Lyly's voice quivered.

"This dumbass demon is trying to use me as a vessel! Help me out here!" Ally coughed into her elbow, waving her other hand, trying to possibly move the flames to make an exit. It didn't work.

"I don't have magic like you! I can't do anything, I'm sorry Ally!" Lyly's ears went down, her lower lip quivered.

"Whatever! Figure something out!" Ally yelled.

She squinted her eyes as she looked around the fire making sure to keep moving so she didn't get swallowed by the flames. Scar's laughter echoed around the entire ring of hot fire. Ally couldn't tell where it was coming from. It felt like it was right next to her, but when she looked, nobody was there.

"Clay! Satoru! Go get help! Please!" Lyly cried out. Hopefully the boys were still on the other side and alive. At least, Ally hoped that Clay was alright.

"Scar! You can't do this! You could accidentally kill them!" Satoru's voice shouted from the other side. His voice sounded shaky, like he was going to break down at any moment.

"You know, Alyson. You could end this right now and nobody else would get hurt!" Scar mused, floating out from the flames in front of her.

"I can see the potential in you but you're holding yourself back! Don't you want to become powerful? I know you do, because who wouldn't?" Scar floated in a circle around Ally clearly trying to intimidate her. After a few moments, she floated in front of Ally in a sitting position in midair with her legs crossed.

"I already told you. I'm not becoming your vessel! I don't want to become super powerful. I don't even care about whatever that Nyx creature is doing! I just want to find my mom and Elliot!" Ally stomped her foot angrily. She wanted to attack Scar so badly, but the flames mixed with Scar made it hard to make out anything. If only there was a way to-

Right as she was in the middle of thinking, her vision started to become blurry. She wobbled slightly forward and tried to regain her balance. What was happening?

"Ally! Are you okay? Ally!" Lyly screamed from somewhere in the room.

Ally didn't reply as her vision continued to swirl in ways that it shouldn't be able to. When it became too much for her, she fell forward.

She was lying face up, she knew that. She just wanted to give up. This honestly felt hopeless but, if she gave in, Scar would use her as a puppet. That was not happening. She couldn't give up. She had to finish this nightmare of a day and then she could drill everyone in Hell about her family's whereabouts.

Ally sat up, but everything looked different. The flames were black, almost everything around her was. There were a few things that were white like Lyly and most of Scar's body, except for her hair. Ally had no clue what was going on but whatever it was it made her job a whole lot easier.

Using her fire powers on the head Fire Demon was probably going to be useless. So, she'd have to get close and hope that she could fend Scar off for a little bit before getting killed or possibly eaten.

Ally stood up glaring at Scar, who was still floating in the air with a look of amusement on her stupid face.

"So, you're using your fancy little powers, huh? They could be stronger if I possessed you, you know," Scar yawned.

"Not gonna happen!" Ally walked up to the Fire Demon, ignoring Lyly's pleas to run. She had been waiting to fight someone for the past couple weeks and Clay stopped her every time. Now, there was nobody there to stop her. Lyly didn't have the guts to get in the way.

Ally reached behind her, grabbing her knife from her bag, while keeping eye contact with the Fire Demon. Then, without thinking, she ran at Scar. She hopped up in the air gripping the handle of her blade tight as she went to stab Scar in the face.

Scar just laughed and grabbed Ally's blade with her teeth, holding onto the sharp end as blood started to leak from her mouth, but Scar didn't seem to care.

Ally palms began to sweat as she tried to shove the knife down the demon's throat, but it wouldn't budge. She heard the snapping of Scar's tail and suddenly she was lifted off the ground, the tail around her throat, holding her breath hostage.

Scar stared calmly at Ally as she struggled. Without a care in the world, she pulled the knife out of her mouth and looked it over. There were a few bite marks on the blade now making it utterly useless. Her mouth was bleeding, but her teeth weren't even chipped.

"See? You couldn't even get a single attack in. I'll hand it to you though, you still had the guts to try and fight me, even though it was pointless! Kudos to you!"

Ally kicked and squirmed clawing at her neck trying to pull the tail off so she could breathe. Her hands felt warm, like they were on fire. When she glanced at her hands, she was surprised to see that they were on fire. It wasn't burning her, so she must have done that herself, not Scar. Scar looked temporarily shocked. Now was her chance.

She bit down on Scar's hand, causing the demon to shriek in pain and alarm. Scar's tail released Ally giving her the chance she needed. Ally grabbed the Fire Demon by the throat and kicked her long legs a few times knocking her onto the ground.

"Hey! Cut that out!" Scar slashed her claws at Ally's face.

Ally moved her head quickly before she could take out an eyeball, but Ally did manage to get cut on her cheek. Ally growled and yanked her knife away from Scar and continued to kick her. Ally's whole body felt like it was on fire. Actually, it was on fire!

She felt the adrenaline kicking in as she kicked, slashed, and punched Scar, not even paying attention to what she was hitting or if she was landing any hits. She just wanted to make Scar suffer. She didn't care what happened afterwards. It looked like two wild animals were attacking each other, each desperate to be victorious.

"Ally! Someone's coming to save us!" Lyly coughed.

Alyson ignored Lyly, continuing to attack Scar brutally. Scar was fighting back as well slashing at Ally with her claws. Neither of them was stopping at this point.

"Ally, come on! We need to go!" Lyly continued to cough, running towards Ally and grabbing her by the bookbag. She was trying to pull Ally away but why?

"What now?!" Ally finally responded. She didn't even bother to look at Lyly. She couldn't let this opportunity go to waste. She had to keep going. More punching. More pain.

"The flames are getting smaller! We can leave now! Please Ally!"

"I'm not done yet!"

Ally went for another swing and started to cough. The smoke around her was really starting to get to her. Maybe she should listen to Lyly for once and escape.

Ally pushed Scar away and stood up, who was just laughing. Geez, this lady was creepy as hell. Ally couldn't believe that she ever wanted to meet another Fire Demon. If they were all like this, she never wanted to interact with another one again.

She turned around slightly to face Lyly, coughing into her elbow.

"...alright Lyly, I think we're done here. We can get going-"

Lyly was on the ground, motionless. The flames around them were smaller, just like Lyly said.

They were small enough to jump over. Though the smoke was still there suffocating their lungs.

"Lyly…?" Ally asked slowly, nudging Lyly with her foot. No response.

"Lyly! Lyly, Answer me! This isn't funny!"

Once again, there was no reply. Did Ally's lack of compassion kill Lyly? No no, that wasn't possible. It was just some smoke, it couldn't have killed Lyly that quickly, right? Right??

Scar was laughing like this was the funniest thing she's ever witnessed. "You killed her! And I thought I was bad!"

Ally's vision went back to normal, and she stared at Lyly, who was not moving. She was too horrified about what she'd done. Lyly was super annoying, but Ally was just starting to consider her a friend and now, she managed to get Lyly killed. This wasn't happening!

"Well, that was fun! I hear the boss, so I'm gonna bounce. But don't forget about my deal. It's never too late to reconsider!" Scar stood up and disappeared in a ball of flames.

Ally heard familiar footsteps rushing towards her, at least three people but she didn't look up. She didn't deserve anything she had. She was a terrible person. Ally deserved whatever fate was coming to her. Maybe a public execution.

She felt someone's arms wrapping around her, hugging her tight. Claymore. He was alright. Thank goodness.

"Ally! What happened?! Are you alri- oh gosh, you're bleeding!" Clay sounded terrified. He didn't let go of Ally.

She looked up to face her brother and the others that followed. Satoru knelt on the ground, poking Lyly lightly. Standing there next to Claymore was the cranky orphanage owner/demon, Sherry.

"Finally. You've arrived. Your father is waiting for you, I suppose." Sherry said coldly, her eyes staring into Ally's soul.

CHAPTER NINE

The Incident

The rest of the walk to the castle was in silence. Clay kept trying to talk to Ally while they walked but she wouldn't look him in the eyes. If she did, Ally knew that she'd start to cry.

"She's not dead, just inhaled too much smoke!" Satoru announced cheerfully. He was holding Lyly with his shadow hands, so she floated alongside him. Her tail was moving slightly, but other than that, she was limp.

Sherry looked behind her at Clay and Ally. "I do apologize for Scar's behavior. She can be a little too enthusiastic when it comes to getting what she wants."

"I'm pretty sure that she tried to kill Ally!" Clay grumbled.

"I know, and I'm sorry about that. It's difficult to keep an eye on all my employees at once."

"My sister almost died! Pay attention to your employees!"

Ally looked up, stunned that Clay was yelling. He didn't usually get angry like this but given the circumstances, she could understand why he was getting so mad. If the roles were reversed, she would be choking Sherry out by now.

Sherry just stared at Clay with no expression on her face. She looked awful, compared to the last time Ally saw her. She had major bags under her eyes and a few scratches on her face.

"I had no way of stopping this. My goal has never been to get either of you injured."

"What about at the orphanage? Your snake nearly killed Ally too!" Clay stomped his foot almost tripping when he walked.

"Remus got too carried away. Also, if I wanted to hurt you, I would have done so, a long time ago. You were under my care for about seven years, and I never tried to harm you two."

"Why didn't you?"

"I wouldn't harm a child without reason. Besides, your father instructed me to keep you both safe while under my care."

Satoru glanced over at Clay making a goofy looking face at him. Clay met his gaze and chuckled a little. That seemed to lighten up Clay's mood.

"We've arrived. Prepare yourselves." Sherry stopped walking suddenly, staring up at the castle in front of them. It was huge, dark and scary looking. It looked like something right out of a horror movie. How original. Except there were some banners by the front gates blowing around in the wind displaying a couple demonic looking symbols.

The drawbridge immediately went down, and the group crossed it, entering the courtyard. Ally took notice of all the demons in armor and basically anybody who walked by. Everyone was so focused on their task until their group approached. The guards stopped and bowed to all of them. Again, with that!? Were demons going to continue doing that whenever they walked around?

"Lord Satoru! You've returned!" A few of the demons gasped. They looked at Satoru with a rush of joy and relief.

Satoru did those stupid finger gun things at the demons and bowed.

"I wasn't going to let one little fight be the end of me! I'm not going anywhere, don't you worry,"

He looked to his side at the unconscious Lyly, who was resting in the shadow hands. "Actually, since you're here. Could one of you take this girl to the infirmary? She inhaled a lot of smoke. I just want to make sure that she's alright."

The demons nodded, and picked Lyly up carefully, walking away with her.

Ally glared at Satoru and grabbed him by the back of his sweater. "You're pushing your luck, Satoru. Care to explain?"

"Your dad will explain sooner or later. Now let me go!"

"No. I want to know now!"

"Alyson Siberia!" Sherry stopped walking and gave her a death stare.

Ally begrudgingly let Satoru go, as a demon guard walked up to them again. He bowed and then faced Sherry.

"Lucifer is waiting in the throne room." The guard announced to Sherry, who nodded.

"We'll be arriving shortly. How are the decorations holding up?"

"Just wonderful. We finally were able to string up the lights in the great hall without Lady Scar attempting to eat them."

The guard smiled at Sherry. The group continued to progress through the courtyard to go inside the castle.

Clay glanced at Satoru while they walked. "Does Scar eat everything?" He muttered.

Satoru shrugged. "Pretty much. I've seen her try to eat spoons before when she's hungry…"

Soon, they were wandering through dark hallways made of stone, lit by lamps overhead. As they walked further, the area got brighter. There were also fewer guards around.

Orange and purple lights were strung on the walls. There was a lot of smoke on the ground, swirling around and turning into smoke versions of the people that walked past. The smoke turned into a life-sized version of Ally. The smoke creature spit at Ally, which just pissed her off.

"Hey! Cut that out!" Ally hissed and smacked at the smoke. Clay looked at the smoke version of Ally and started to laugh a bit.

"It's harmless Ally. Nothing to worry about! I think..." Clay chuckled, and patted Ally on the shoulder. At this point, anything in this place could be harmful. She had to be careful, remain alert and not get too starstruck about the demon world they were in.

"Sherry! Is that you down there?" A voice yelled from further down the hall, making the entire hallway shake. Sherry looked at the end of the hallway and gestured for the kids to keep following her.

"Yes Lord Lucifer. And I brought some guests along with me." Sherry answered back, shouting slightly.

"Lucifer? As in, our father, Lucifer?" Clay gulped. Satoru nodded nervously at Claymore in response.

Ally didn't waste any time after getting that confirmation. She ran right through the smoke version of herself, which swirled around her, and tore through it. Ally ignored Sherry's yells for her to turn back. She could hear her brother and the other two demons running after her, but she didn't care. She wanted answers about the whereabouts of her brother and mother. And who would know best of all? Her father. Besides, Scar said to ask him. She did agree with Scar on that despite Ally not being fond of her at all.

Ally ran right into the throne room ahead of Sherry and froze. A man around seven feet tall was standing there with his arms crossed and his red eyes narrowed.

This man reminded her greatly of Claymore in the face but older and scary looking.

The man had medium length dark brown, nearly black hair that was wavy, with two red streaks. One on the left side, one on the right. Large horns about the length of Ally's entire arm were on his head in his neatly done hair. He had a thin beard with scratches on various parts of his face. He wore a dark red button up shirt with one of the buttons undone near his neck, black pants with a silver belt and a long black royal cape on his shoulders. He was wearing gray boots that had blood stains by the heels, and he had a demonic tail that touched the floor and dragged around. Lucifer himself was staring her down. Her own father.

As he stared at her, a judgmental frown appeared on his face. What the hell was his problem? He was the one that never showed up or told his own children that he existed!

Ally gritted her teeth and glared at her father. "What's your problem, huh old man?!"

"Sherry. Who is this?" Lucifer asked in a calm tone, despite his facial expression. He didn't move a muscle. He just stared at Ally.

Sherry ran out from the hallway with Clay and Satoru at her heels. She gave Ally a slight look of annoyance, before looking up at Lucifer, and bowing.

"Your daughter, Alyson and your oldest son, Claymore, have arrived," Sherry responded, paused, then spoke again. "Also, Satoru is back."

Lucifer crossed his arms, nodding. "I can see that…None of them caused any trouble, did they?"

"Besides destroying half of my orphanage in the human world, they managed to get on Scar's bad side already."

"Ah, I see. You were supposed to watch over them from the safety of the human world, why are they down here?"

Satoru's tail snapped at the air behind him, and he took a step forward. "Sir, I think you should listen to what your kids have to say, along with Sherry and me. They came all the way down here, to see you, and warn you about what's to come-"

Lucifer waved his hand, and Satoru went silent. "Preposterous. If you're talking about Nyx, we defeated that creature seven years ago. It's not coming back, and none of you are going to convince me otherwise."

Ally's left eye twitched. He definitely knew what happened at their house. Seven years ago, Nyx attacked their house. She was so close to getting the full story, but nobody wanted to share. Guess she'd have to force him to tell.

"Listen up Lucifer. I don't give two shits about what happens to your kingdom. I didn't even know you were my dad, which, by the way, I'm never calling you that, until Death herself appeared out of nowhere and told me! I only came down here so I could find out what happened to our mom and brother! Now you're going to tell me, or I'll burn this place to the ground!"

Sherry's eyes widened slightly. "Alyson Siberia! Watch your tone while talking to Lucifer-"

"I don't care who he is! He's nothing to me!" Ally's hands began to heat up and then flames appeared in both of her hands.

Clay stared at Ally, looking worried. "Ally, I don't think you should resort to violence this quickly!"

Ally looked at her brother and her eyes softened slightly. Last time she let her rage take over one of her friends almost died. She didn't think she could bear it if Clay got hurt because she was having a temper tantrum. He was all she had left.

She waved her hands, and the flames went out. Ally didn't look at anybody else but Clay. Sherry coughed, which caused Alyson to stare at her.

"Sir, with all due respect. I think that your children deserve to know what happened. After everything they've been through to get here, and in general," Sherry sighed.

Ally was stunned. Why was Sherry sticking up for them? They trashed her orphanage and Sherry hated Ally! At least, that's what it always felt like.

Lucifer looked stunned as well, and he tried to stop her. "I don't think-"

"It's a smart idea. We've been keeping this from them for far too long. They have the right to know what happened that night." Sherry nodded, staring Lucifer down.

The devil stared right back at her. They were silent for a moment until Lucifer looked away and grumbled.

"Fine… But they better not get mad at me when they see what happened." Lucifer crossed his arms. Sherry looked semi-proud of herself.

"Keep your mouths shut." Sherry said softly and waved her arms in a swirling motion in the air.

Ally looked over at Clay and Satoru. Sure enough, they were both silent. Lucifer took a few steps back.

The air around them started to feel cold like they just stepped into a freezer. Then, everything got really bright, and all Ally could see was bright white. It hurt her eyes, so she shut them. She didn't say a word. She didn't know what was happening.

When she opened her eyes, she wasn't in Lucifer's castle anymore. She was standing in her old living room. It was raining outside, the thunder sounded violent. The floor felt squishy, probably because of the wet carpet she was standing on. How did she get here? What did Sherry do?

Ally turned her head towards Sherry, who was standing in a corner, holding her hands together in a praying position.

"What are you doing? Are you praying for our downfall?" Ally asked her casually.

Sherry stared at Ally; blank faced. "I'm holding this memory open and if you want to see what happened that night, then I suggest you stop teasing me."

Satoru tapped Ally on the shoulder. She turned around and narrowed her eyes at him. "Oh, come on, don't be like that! At least now, you'll get all the answers to your millions of questions,"

"You're still suspicious and I don't trust you..." She growled.

"Yeah yeah, whatever you say, Ally."

Clay was staring at the living room couch. He hadn't said a word since they got there. He looked like he was in a trance. Ally walked over to him to see what he was looking at. Her eyes widened, and she immediately understood why Claymore was being so quiet and still.

"It's alright, the thunder stopped Ally," A boy said calmly.

The boy was kneeling in front of the couch, muttering to himself. No wait, he was talking to somebody that was behind the couch. He said something else, and a little girl ran out from behind the couch.

It was her. Though, not Ally now. Ally when she was a little girl. And that boy, it was a younger version of Claymore. He looked happier, more carefree and relaxed. She was too freaked out by the situation to listen to the conversation that Young Ally and Young Clay were having.

Ally looked at Clay, who had the same freaked out look on his face that Ally probably had. "What the hell is this?"

Satoru walked in between the siblings and tried to poke Young Clay's head. His hand went right through his head, and

170

Young Clay didn't even seem to notice Satoru. Nor did the present-day versions of Clay and Ally, standing mere feet from him.

"It's just a memory. They can't see you, you're just along for the ride, basically." Satoru's tail swished around as he talked.

The younger versions of Clay and Ally exited the living room walking into the dining room. Young Ally pulled her chair out and hopped onto it, while Young Clay pushed it in for her. Whatever Young Ally was talking about clearly made her excited. She was smiling at her brother with nuggets in her mouth.

Now Ally remembered. She had been excited for her birthday, which according to this memory, was tomorrow.

"You still do that," Clay pointed out.

Ally looked at Clay, confused. "Do what?"

"Talk with your mouth full." He snickered.

"I do not!"

While the present-day Clay and Ally bickered, the door of the house opened in the background, causing both of them to jump and look at the front door.

"Alyson! Claymore! We're home!" The familiar voice of their mother called, as she walked into their line of vision, their brother Elliot right at her side.

The memory versions began talking to each other happily, while the real versions stared at their mother and brother. Both had tears in their eyes. Ally didn't want to cry. She hated crying but she couldn't help it. Seeing her mother and brother again after all these years was too much for her to handle right now.

Clay stared at the ground and started to cry. He just didn't want Ally to see him cry. That was understandable, as Ally was attempting and failing to do the same thing.

Cora's amber yellow eyes looked so full of life, though there was a hint of worry in them that Ally never noticed before. Maybe because when she was with her mother, she didn't look for signs of distress. Ally had always assumed that their mother would be around forever. At the bare minimum, at least until their thirties or forties.

As Clay, Ally, and Satoru watched the scene unfold, Young Clay was now speaking to both Young Ally and Elliot about their birthdays. Apparently, Ally had been too focused on her mom to realize that more events were taking place before her eyes.

"Alright you two. It's time to get to bed." Young Clay patted his siblings on their heads.

Elliot smiled and ran off to his room, excited to turn eight years old the next day. He was the sweetest little boy. He would zone out sometimes and not pay attention to her when she was talking. Despite that, she was proud to have Elliot as her twin brother.

Young Ally stuck her tongue out at Young Clay and crossed her arms. Even at a young age, Ally was stubborn. Ally was old enough to admit that she could be a pain sometimes.

"I don't wanna go to bed yet!" Young Ally whined.

"Alyson, you can't stay up, you'll be so tired tomorrow that you'll sleep through your birthday. You wouldn't want that, would you?" Young Clay chuckled.

As he said that, Young Ally stood there in thought for a moment, before replying again. "Ok! I'll go to bed then. Can you tuck me in? Please?"

Young Clay smiled at his little sister and nodded. "Sure Al, I'll get you to bed."

He picked up Young Ally and started walking towards her room but stopped when he saw his mother still standing in front of the window.

Ally noticed that their mother had been standing by the front window, ever since she arrived home. Though Ally didn't take note of this behavior when she was little, she was paying attention now. She had to know the full truth about what happened that night. This was probably her only chance to ever see this again.

"I'll meet you in your bedroom to tuck you in, okay Ally?" Young Clay set Young Ally down gently and watched her run down the hallway towards her room. Then, he drew his attention back to his mother. "Mom?"

Cora didn't say anything as she continued to stare out the window, watching the rain pour down on the sidewalk outside.

"Mom! It's late, what are you doing? You're starting to worry me…" Young Clay muttered, which got Cora's attention.

She turned and faced Young Clay, a faraway look in her eyes. She knew something bad was going to happen. Ally could see it in her eyes.

"Have I ever told you about your father before, Claymore?" Cora whispered.

"No, you haven't. You told us that he left us-"

"He was such a kind and caring man. Dark brown, almost black hair. It suited him well. You look so much like him, and you don't even know it," Cora smiled at Clay, and put her hands together. "I think he would be very happy if he met you someday."

Young Clay nodded. "How come you're bringing him up now?" He asked his mother, who blinked like she had forgotten what he had asked for a second.

"Oh! That…" Cora sighed deeply, kneeling in front of Young Clay, and giving him a long hug. "You need to listen to me closely, and do as I say, got it?"

Ally looked alarmed. She looked at Clay to see what his reaction was, but his eyes were closed tight. What was that about? It was just a hug!

Before Young Clay, or Cora said anything more thunder clashed, and lightning flashed making them both jump. They looked out the front window staring at a tree nearby. It was rocking back and forth, smoke coming out from the side of it. The large tree looked as if it were going to fall at any second. And when it did, it would fall right on top of Young Clay and her mother.

"Mom, that tree is going to come through the window!" Young Clay yelped and pointed at the tree, which slowly began to fall towards the window. Cora's eyes widened, staring at the tree, frozen where she stood. Now Ally realized why Clay had his eyes shut.

Young Clay grabbed his mother's hand and started running towards his sibling's room, which was at the other end of the house. But he didn't make it very far, before the tree collapsed into the living room.

With a loud crash, the tree fell through their home, pieces of ceiling and broken furniture flying everywhere. Cora let go of her son's hand and pushed him forward, so he wasn't as close to the tree as Cora was about to be. Young Clay stumbled forward and tripped on a glass shard, his entire body slamming onto the ground. His hand fell on the glass, cutting it slightly.

The poor boy looked ready to faint, but he didn't. He looked behind him, his mother lay on the ground, her legs pinned underneath a tree branch. The side of her head was bleeding. She seemed to be knocked out. Hopefully, she was just knocked out.

Ally felt her arms starting to shake. She knew what was coming next. She didn't want to watch it happen again; while standing there helplessly but she had no choice.

"Mom!" Young Clay crawled over to Cora and shook her. She didn't move, but Ally could see that she was breathing. Young Clay continued to shake her to attempt and wake her up, to no avail.

"Claymore!" Two small voices yelled, sounding far away. Though, the yells got louder, as Young Ally and Elliot ran out from their bedrooms down the hallway towards their brother.

Elliot was in tears, looking at the scene before him. Young Ally's eyes were watering, but she wasn't crying yet. She was close to bawling her eyes out. Ally remembered that feeling.

"W-we heard something crash, so we came to check on you!" Elliot sniffled. Ally remembered this conversation. Elliot had come running into her room, crying. At the time she had been confused, she had almost fallen asleep waiting for Clay to tuck her in. Once she had heard her brother calling out to their mother, she quickly got out of bed.

"Oh guys, you aren't hurt, right?" Young Clay stopped shaking Cora and sat up. He looked at his little siblings and put his hand on both of their cheeks, looking extremely worried.

"No, we're okay but, you're not! Your hand is bleeding!" Young Ally exclaimed, with a look of horror on her face. Her voice sounded like it was starting to break, as the tears started to flow down her cheeks.

"I'll be alright, it was just some glass," Young Clay said quickly, then looked at their mother. "I don't think we have the strength to move that tree... We need to get the police. They can help us. Let's get going." The twins nodded.

Clay walked up to the young versions of their family and knelt. He was looking tearfully at Elliot. Ally felt horrible, but she didn't know what to say. She wasn't good at comforting, that was usually Clay's department but, she should try, he needed it.

Ally walked over to Clay quietly about to attempt and hug him but before she got the chance, she noticed something was wrong with the scene before them. Young Clay was staring outside through the hole that the fallen tree made. There was something walking towards them at an alarming speed.

Young Ally and Elliot took notice of this too, their eyes widened with fear. They didn't know what to do, neither did Young Clay. Nobody moved, not even Clay, Ally, and Satoru.

"Kids, you need to run…" Cora's voice whispered softly. Her eyes were open slightly, she looked worried.

"No mom! We can't leave you!" Elliot cried, grabbing his mother's arm and attempting to pull her out from under the tree. It didn't do anything. He was too weak.

Ally watched in silence, as the creature ran inside the house. She recognized the creature from her nightmares who she now knew was called Nyx. This creature's presence stuck with her over these past seven years.

"I love all of you, run now, please!" Cora shouted with the last of her energy, before going silent again.

Young Clay stared at the creature as its giant wings flapped, soaring right at Cora. It grabbed a branch from the fallen tree, holding it close to the woman's face. Nyx's singular eye stared at Cora, not turning its gaze for a second. Then, it happened.

Cora looked over at her children with tears in her eyes, as Nyx drove the branch right through Cora's head, coming out the other side. Ally could see various bits of brain sticking out from the back of her mother's head, and other things that Ally didn't have the stomach to describe.

The younger versions of themselves didn't say a word. Young Clay had his hands covering his sibling's eyes, even though they already witnessed their mother being murdered. They were too scared to do anything but stare at the creature that took their mother's life away. The only thing that could be heard was the wind coming through the hole in the house and the rain outside.

Nyx laughed. A low, cruel sounding laugh. That sound would haunt Ally for the rest of her life. It didn't appear to feel any guilt that it just murdered someone's mother, right in front of her young children.

Nyx laughed to itself, swinging the corpse around like a wrecking ball, still attached to the branch. Nyx's mouth wasn't very visible, but Ally could see a cruel grin on its face.

Young Clay shook his head. He had so many tears in his eyes that Ally was surprised that he could see anything. He grabbed his sibling's hands and ran as fast as he could towards the front door.

The second that he started running, he realized he had made a terrible mistake. Nyx wasn't happy with his decision. Ally, Clay, and Satoru stood there in utter silence, watching as Nyx scurried after the little kids grabbing chairs with its tentacles and throwing the sharp bits at them.

Young Clay tried his best to shield his younger siblings without getting himself killed, but Ally could see how difficult it was for him. His heart was probably pounding out of his chest. Ally remembered that hers was that day.

Nyx screamed and started ripping at the walls as it made its way towards the kids. The trio were at the front door now, which seemed to be locked shut.

"Claymore, the door is stuck!" Elliot whisper shouted. He tugged at the door handle, but it wouldn't budge.

Young Ally pushed Elliot out of the way and pulled at the door as well, a desperate look in her eyes. "We're trapped! Clay, what do we do?"

Young Clay stared at his siblings, then at Nyx. Then back at Young Ally and Elliot again. The tears were getting heavier, he could barely see what was in front of him. He was trembling, his voice was so shaky, and his breathing was sped up, and frantic.

"I-I-...I don't know! I don't know, I'm sorry!"

Nyx caught up to them, taking Young Clay's weakness as a perfect time to strike. It reached forward with its twisted hand, about to grab Young Clay by the back of the throat.

Once again, Ally looked over at Clay. He had his eyes shut. This time though, he was hiding behind Satoru. Satoru wasn't saying anything. He was softly patting Clay's head with his tail, while Satoru watched the scene before him unfold.

Elliot looked at Nyx with a terrified expression but found enough strength and bravery to shove Young Clay into the wall, out of harm's way. Young Ally ducked down and curled up into a ball, shielding her head with her hands. She was crying her heart out at this point. She felt so weak and helpless.

Nyx grinned through its goo and grabbed Elliot by the throat. It squeezed. The sound of cracking bones filled the air. Elliot kicked and squirmed with all his might but there wasn't anything he could do.

Young Clay grabbed Young Ally and pulled her out of harm's way. Ally knew that he wanted to save Elliot too, but he was too scared. She had felt the same way, after all.

The clock in the kitchen chimed twelve, as Elliot's body fell to the ground, motionless. It was now the next day, Elliot, and Ally's birthday who both were turning eight years old. Elliot would never age past that.

"E-elliot, I'm so sorry…" Young Clay whimpered, with another shaky breath. He led his little sister into the kitchen. It hadn't been destroyed yet, unlike the rest of their house.

It was a typical kitchen with a fridge, oven, cabinets containing food, plates, and other kitchenware. They had a large cabinet that was tall enough to hide in. That's where mom kept the iron and sometimes spare chairs.

"In the cabinet, hurry!" Young Clay whispered to Young Ally. It was their only chance. They couldn't escape the house any other way. The only exit door was blocked and if they went through the hole in the house, that would involve passing up Nyx. They both knew that if they went near Nyx again, it would rip them to pieces.

Young Clay opened the door moving the spare chairs so they could both hide. Young Ally jumped inside, and Young Clay followed. Ally couldn't see what was going on inside, but she remembered it all too well. She was hugging her brother like her life depended on it, trying to resist the urge to cry or scream for help. Clay had covered his mouth to cover up his loud breathing, he had been shaking so badly. Ally thought he was going to fall to pieces at that moment.

Just then, Nyx entered the kitchen, staring at the ceiling. Did it not know where the kids were hiding? Was it stupid? Why was it standing there?

Gooey tentacles popped out of its back. Those tentacles grabbed at anything that wasn't attached to the ground which basically was everything that was in the kitchen.

Nyx started throwing everything around in a fit of absolute rage, including the cabinet that Young Ally and Clay were hiding in. Now Ally knew what all that banging was outside.

The cabinet smashed into bits against the wall. The door opened and the siblings fell out. Both were knocked out cold from the impact.

Nyx noticed this and walked towards them. Before it could do anything, a demon appeared in between them, his hands outstretched in a protective stance. It was a familiar demon, with long jet-black hair and cherry red eyes. He was wearing that same vintage sweater and gray jeans. His tail was snapping at the air around him, his eyes filled with rage, and a bit of nervousness. He looked slightly younger than he did now in the face, and more serious looking.

"Clay, open your eyes!" Ally nudged Clay, who still had his eyes closed.

Clay opened his eyes, and stared in amazement at the Young Satoru, protecting the knocked-out siblings. "Satoru?"

Satoru looked at Clay and gave him a little smile. "I was protecting you both. I told you that I would never hurt either of you."

Ally scoffed. At least she finally got the clear evidence that Satoru wasn't trying to do anything bad. In fact, that day he was the only thing in between death taking them away to an early grave.

Nyx's head tilted to the left and kept tilting until it was resting on its own shoulder. It looked confused.

Young Satoru waved his hand quickly and a shadowy hand formed, pushing Nyx away from them. It was a bit violent, as Nyx was shoved into the kitchen wall. Ally loved seeing that creature get what was coming to it.

Nyx hissed and an army of gooey hands reached forward towards the Shadow Demon. Luckily, Young Satoru was prepared.

He was able to quickly counter the attack with more shadow hands. Each shadow hand grabbed the gooey Nyx hand and pushed it back with all its strength. Young Satoru yawned, that wasn't good. Satoru got tired very easily from using his powers. At least that's how it worked in the present. Apparently, it was always a thing for him because Young Satoru looked like he was going to fall asleep soon despite not being there for very long.

Nyx saw this as its chance and grabbed the fridge with another long tentacle. Nyx cackled, as the fridge flew right at Young Satoru and slammed into him. It knocked him to the side and sent him tumbling into the wall. It looked like he had gotten crushed by the fridge, but Young Satoru's hand was sticking out on the side. He pushed it off himself slowly. There was already blood on his sweater and coming out from the side of his mouth.

The creature sat on the ground, as the goo started quickly traveling across the entire kitchen floor. Young Satoru's eyes widened slightly with worry, but it was quickly replaced with a smug look. He waved both his hands and stood on top of the broken fridge. A pair of shadow hands appeared and lifted both Young Clay and Young Ally off the ground and safely held them towards the ceiling.

Nyx screamed, grabbing pieces of broken wood, and throwing them at Young Satoru. The wood chunks flew at Young Satoru. He only had a second to react. Ally didn't know how he'd be able to get out of there safely, especially with all the goo on the ground.

Young Satoru jumped from countertop to countertop, barely missing the wood as it flew at him. Some of the pieces ended up hitting him, stabbing into Young Satoru's arms and some pieces of wood were lodged into the wall behind him as he moved around. Despite the fact that the pieces of wood in his arms were small, they still had to hurt and judging by Young Satoru's expression, it definitely was causing some pain.

Nyx laughed and stumbled towards Young Satoru. As it approached, the goo from the floor began to rise, like grass growing, but sped up. And then, it lunged forward, attacking Young Satoru from all sides. He stopped running on the countertops and fell to his knees, holding his hands outstretched on either side of himself. The moment before the goo would have latched onto him, a ball of shadows formed around him just in time. Nyx screeched something again, but Ally wasn't paying attention to it right now. She was focused on Young Satoru. He looked frightened, scared for his life as he desperately tried to keep up his shadow shield. One false move and he'd become corrupted.

"Um, Satoru?" Ally found herself saying, not taking her eyes off the scene before her.

"Yes Ally?" Satoru asked. His voice was quieter than usual, more delicate sounding.

"I'm sorry."

"For?"

"For blaming you and calling you a jerk. I can see that you risked your life for us. I should have been more grateful, but I am now."

Satoru was quiet for a moment. Ally was nervous that he wasn't going to accept her apology. She felt weird whenever she told someone she was sorry. The words didn't feel natural to her. She knew that sounded terrible, but it was the truth.

"It's alright. Don't stress about it too much!" Satoru exclaimed after a few moments of silence between him and Ally.

Thank goodness, he accepted it. Now, she just needed to apologize to one more person. Lyly. If she was awake by the time they were done with this memory and talking to Lucifer she might. No, Ally would make the time to apologize. She had to!

Ally was snapped back to focus when she heard screaming coming from the memory. She looked back at Young Satoru and gasped. Something had gotten through the shadow shield. A couple of wood chunks managed to get to Young Satoru and were sticking out from his gut.

Young Satoru's shield started to falter, his eyes threatening to close. He kept his hands up even though his arms were shaking from the pain.

Nyx's dog ears twitched. It heard something that made its eye widen a bit. It stopped trying to attack Young Satoru, its ears staying up on high alert.

Ally was confused. She didn't hear anything. What was Nyx looking around for? Her question was answered for her almost immediately, when she looked outside through the hole in the living room. A familiar demon was approaching, holding onto a tall snake made of glass. A demon with long layered silver hair, and cornflower blue eyes. How did Nyx hear her coming?

"Madam Siberia!" Memory Sherry called as she walked into the house. She had her usual disappointed expression on which Ally wasn't surprised to see. Her pet snake's tail rattled as they approached.

Once Memory Sherry entered the house, Nyx seemingly melted into the floor, joining the goop already on the floor. Quickly, it swirled around on the floor, going into the hallway by the front door. Wait a second. Elliot's body was there.

Clay and Ally seemed to have the same thought at the same time, because they both ran after the goo. It was weird, they were able to walk on the goo in the memory without being affected. Though, it did feel cold. Probably because it was just a memory, and not the real thing.

They both stopped in the doorway, just in time to see Elliot's body get covered with the corruption goo and disappeared out of sight. He had died for basically nothing. He was only eight years old and should have lived.

Clay knelt and stared at the floor. "His body, it-"

"I know Clay. I know." Ally interrupted him. She didn't want to hear it. She didn't want to cry.

"What about mom…?"

"I don't know."

And with that cheerful exchange, the siblings rushed into the living room, following the goo as it made its way there as well. There were two Sherrys in the living room now. The memory one, who was holding onto her snake, so she didn't step on the corruption goo, and Sherry from the present, who was still in the corner of the room. She hadn't moved this whole time, and she still had her hands in a praying position. Her eyes were closed, deep in concentration.

The Memory Sherry, present Clay, and Ally watched in horror as the corruption goo made its way towards Cora's body and swallowed her whole as well. Then, it melted into the floor. Gone. Like it had never been there.

The siblings stared at the floor in silence, as the Memory Sherry let go of her snake and began pacing around the living room, examining the wrecked home.

"Satoru... He got stabbed!" Clay exclaimed and ran out of the living room. Ally didn't understand why he was so worried about Young Satoru, it was just a memory. It's not like they didn't know what was going to happen to him or anything. Nonetheless, Ally followed her big brother back into the kitchen.

When they arrived, there wasn't any corruption in the kitchen anymore. Young Satoru's shadow hands had disappeared and the younger versions of themselves were laying on the floor by the wall both unconscious.

Young Satoru himself was slumped over nearby Young Clay and Ally. He was coughing up a ton of blood, more than the average human could ever lose. However, he was a demon, so maybe they had more blood?

Memory Sherry didn't seem to notice the boy struggling to live in the other room, she was too focused on her thoughts. Young Satoru still had the wood chunks in his gut which was the cause of more blood exiting his body. He kept closing his eyes for a moment then opening them slowly.

He looked over at Young Clay, who was closer to him. He seemed to be thinking about something in his head. He nodded and reached forward.

"I-it's the only way, I'm sorry…" Young Satoru muttered, placing his hand gently on Young Claymore's forehead.

He started muttering to himself more, Ally couldn't understand what he was saying. It didn't sound like it was in English to her. The house shook violently, the faster Young Satoru spoke. His form began to flicker, from being a solid being to being a small mass of shadows, with no visible form. Eventually his form changed completely to shadows. Young Clay's head was tilted upwards slightly, his eyelids peeled open, despite him still being unconscious. The mass of shadows swarmed him, going right into his eyes. It was a horrifying sight to say the least.

Once the entire mass of shadows was gone, the house stopped shaking. Memory Sherry glanced into the room to see what the commotion was about, but the only thing left of Young Satoru's presence was bloody wood chunks on the ground lying in a pool of blood.

The air began to feel cold again. They were going to get thrown out of the memory any second, there was nothing more to show.

"Bark!"

Ally froze. What was that? A bark? Was there a dog nearby? Maybe the neighbor's dog? Oh, she hoped it didn't get hurt. She liked that dog as a little kid. Ally used to pet her through the fence in the backyard as she was always outside.

A small white dog came running into the kitchen out of nowhere. It was the neighbor's dog after all. She didn't look hurt to Ally, which was a relief.

The dog looked at the unconscious children on the ground, and her ears went down. She laid on the ground in between Young Clay and Ally and closed her eyes.

Memory Sherry nodded and began to approach the unconscious kids and the dog. Ally could hear sirens in the background, but Sherry wasn't fazed by them. She bent down and picked up both children effortlessly and began to leave the ruins of the house silently, the little dog following right behind Sherry.

Before Ally could question anything further, everything got bright again, and they were all transported out of the memory.

CHAPTER TEN

Trial of the Century

As they were transported out of the memory, Clay made sure to keep his eyes shut. Last time he made the mistake of keeping them open, never again.

Clay thought about what he had just experienced for now the second time in his life. He was in too much shock to question how Sherry was able to make that happen. He was also relieved that Satoru hadn't had a hand in anything bad that night.

He thought about what happened when Nyx fled. That thing seemed so frightened by Sherry's presence, maybe it knew that Sherry worked for Lucifer? Sherry did look intimidating, but surely a creature such as Nyx, could have taken her out in an instant.

His mom Cora and Elliot's body were swallowed by the goo. No wonder when they had woken up, they found their other family members missing. The only other living beings in that house had been himself, Ally, and the white dog that was lying beside them.

And of course, the literal kidnapping of himself and his sister. What the hell was that? Sherry just grabbed them and left? Did society know what happened? He had heard sirens, so a neighbor probably called the police. What ever happened with that? He was never told about the authorities showing up. Claymore had so many questions that he wanted to ask but he couldn't get the words out.

Clay shuttered. He didn't want to think about the incident any more than he had to. He kind of knew what had happened, but that wasn't good enough for him. He was supposed to focus on the other mission before it was too late, which was convincing his newfound father that Nyx was going to try and kill him tonight at the Halloween party. However, he wanted his own answers too.

Claymore opened his eyes when he felt himself warming up a bit. He was standing in the throne room again. His sister, Satoru, and Sherry had all returned. They were standing in the same places that they were before they had been shot into that memory.

The only thing different now is that Lucifer wasn't standing in the same place. He was pacing around the room not looking at any of them. Guess he didn't realize that the memory was over and that they were all back.

"What the…" Clay muttered to himself, looking at his sister. Ally was standing there with her eyes fixed on Lucifer. She looked ready to strangle him. Why did she always look ready to hurt people? They just got back. What beef did she have with him already?

"Why didn't you try to save us?! What kind of a father are you? Sending your employees to rescue your family, instead of doing it yourself?!" Ally balled her fists.

Satoru put his hands up, glancing at Claymore. That look in his eyes, he was expecting Clay to say something to calm her down. But in all honesty, he couldn't think of anything.

Lucifer scoffed and put his hand on his hip. "I was doing what was best for the kingdom. If something had happened to me, Hell would be in ruins!"

"What about your family? Did none of that matter to you?"

"Of course it mattered! Why do you think I sent my most trusted demons to rescue you from that place?" Lucifer spat. He was gritting his teeth a lot now. Clay could see his fangs.

Clay thought that was the end of it and so did Ally, but he just kept talking, his voice was getting louder and louder.

"Why do you think I had Sherry place you and your sister in the orphanage? Or, for another thing, why do you think I made sure Lyly went there with you both as well? For your protection!" The devil glared at Ally.

Wait. Did he say…Lyly? Clay didn't think that she was a part of any of this! How could she be? She was just his friend from the orphanage who just so happened to be a mythical creature, right?

Before Ally or anyone else could interrupt him, Clay spoke up. "You- what? What does Lyly have to do with any of this?"

Lucifer paused and looked briefly at Sherry, who didn't have any expression on her face. "I hired Lyly to watch over you and the family when the twins were born. I realized the danger that I was putting you all in, it was safer that way."

"What? That doesn't make any sense! Wouldn't she have been two or something?" Clay ruffled his eyebrows.

This was already starting to get to him. At least he got his answer about Sherry kidnapping them and how they ended up in the orphanage but now he had questions about Lyly too and he knew damn well that nobody wanted to answer them.

Lo and behold, Lucifer was beating around the bush with his reply. "I- it's complicated Claymore. Right now, isn't the time to worry about it. What matters now is that you know what happened to your mother and brother. That's what you all wanted, right?"

Clay really wanted to continue talking about this further, but Lucifer was right. Nyx was still coming to Hell tonight and Lucifer wasn't convinced that it was back in the first place. They had to tell him what was going to happen. Clay didn't know what would happen if Lucifer himself had to fight Nyx.

"As um, comforting it was to know what happened. That's not the only reason we're here. And I think you know the other reason for why we came." Clay fidgeted with his hands as he spoke.

"Now if you're here to tell me that Nyx is coming, I'm going to have to ask you to leave." Lucifer looked over at the hallway they had come through previously. Neither Ally nor Clay were going to go down without a fight.

"For crying out loud, can't you see what's about to happen? Nyx is still a threat!" Ally snarled.

Lucifer shook his head in annoyance. "Well, nobody has seen it since the day that I lost your mother and brother-"

"What does that have to do with anything? It didn't die that day! Half of my damn family did!" Ally interrupted quickly, shutting him down before he could get another word out. Clay was proud of Ally at that moment for sticking up for them.

"We saw in that memory, Nyx just scurried away! It wasn't defeated, it almost killed Satoru!" Clay exclaimed, gesturing to Satoru, who gave Clay a nervous smile.

"That's what I was trying to tell you for years, sir." Sherry said softly, continuing to stare at her boss with no emotion on her face. It was rather creepy.

"Tsk… Even if Nyx was still around, why would it come to Hell? You don't have any proof that it's coming to get me!" Lucifer stomped his foot. The ground where he stepped catching fire for a split second, then it went right back out.

"Proof, you say? There's no proof?!" A familiar voice laughed from behind him.

No. Not now. Anybody but her-

Clay turned around quickly to find that the structure of the throne room had changed slightly. There was a new set of stairs, right above the entrance to the throne room where they had entered through. Clay was confused on how those new stairs appeared, but his confusion only grew when he realized that they were a bright, bubbling orange. Literally, there were bubbles popping on the stairs. The more he stared at them, the less sense it was making to him. These stairs seemed to be made from pure lava, as it was dripping onto the floor and scorching the ground. A railing was on the sides of the stairs, the lava holding those in place. It looked like it had been melted and twisted to create such railings.

Standing at the top of the stairs, looking very proud of herself, was the Fire Demon Scar. Her apparel had changed since the last time he saw her. It was more formal wear this time than her ringmaster outfit she was in when they first met. Scar wore a black and red lace up vest, with a black mini skirt. There was also a long and swishy looking skirt attached in the back.

The demon had black high boots on this time, guess she wanted to change up the color. She had red and orange bits of glitter around her normal eye, that shinned as bright as the flames of her hair. The eye that had an orb in it, was covered with a black eyepatch, decorated with various mini red jewels.

She had a delighted grin on her face as she looked down at everyone, as if they were all inferior to her. Everyone else was silent, unsure of what she was going to do.

Her mallet was held tightly in her hand, as she held it over her shoulder resting, she stared at everyone.

Ally tapped her foot a couple times on the ground and tugged at Clay's sleeve. Clay didn't notice it at first until she started trying to tear his sleeve off.

"What?" Clay whispered, not looking at Ally.

"Hide me! Now!" Ally hissed back.

Clay took a second to process what she said and then stood in front of All. He wasn't fully sure what was happening as Scar made flames circle around Clay, Ally, and Lyly. Judging by Ally's tone and expression, it wasn't good. Maybe that's why she wanted to hide from Scar so badly now.

"I love a good fight! And you know where some fights happen? On the court floor!" Scar cheered, spinning around in a circle happily. Court floor? What was Scar talking about?

Sherry's eye twitched slightly. Seems this happened often. "Scar, this isn't a good time,"

"Hi Sherry! How's it going?" Scar completely ignored what Sherry said and ran down the stairs towards them. The flames of her hair roared and blew around as she ran but they didn't go out.

"I was having a conversation Scar, not now-"

"Good to hear! Well anyways, I heard about your little problem! And I want to help solve it, in a fun way!"

"A fun way? What are you planning, Scar?" Sherry raised an eyebrow at the Fire Demon, who just giggled some more at Sherry's expense.

"A trial! Of Luci, vs the kids! Who's in the right? Who's in the wrong? Only time, and the jury, will tell!"

Lucifer looked annoyed at being referred to as Luci, but he didn't say anything to Scar. He just nodded in agreement to what she had proposed.

"What? Oh, you can't be serious!" Satoru sighed.

Scar ignored his words and slid past everyone else. The flames around Clay, Ally and Lyly went out around them. Scar looked like she was zoned out, or so Clay thought.

The Fire Demon hugged her mallet close and began to sway back and forth, her tail snapping at the air. Her footsteps were soft, and the material of her shoes tapped lightly on the floor.

She continued to sway, until she suddenly paused, holding her free hand out to the side in a stylish manner, as if she was going to take someone's hand and dance with them. As she stood there with her hand out, she threw her mallet into the air with her other hand. It spun slowly above her as it rose towards the ceiling. Her arm was still in the air from throwing the mallet, and she looked up at it, a cheerful smile on her face. Clay was amused by how much she smiled, since he met her there wasn't a time that she looked down or worn out. She kept up her performance as long as someone was around to witness it.

Scar flicked her wrists, as lava flowed out of her palms rapidly, quickly covering the ground. The lava bubbled and began to rise and spread around the room. Scar didn't seem too bothered about this as she continued to dance by herself. Her mallet began to fall right towards her again. In fact, she seemed pleased by it. Excited even.

The lava spread across the entire floor making little circles around the people in the room, so they didn't get burned in the process. Clay didn't know what Scar was trying to do.

Lucifer's throne, a large black chair made of skeletons popped out of the ground, as a lava table rose in front of it. Two more chairs and another table came into being next to Lucifer's. On the right of the tables was a leather red bench.

At least six people could sit there if they wanted to. In the center of the room, a stage formed with a singular leather black chair with wheels on the end and a small wooden table next to it. The table looked like it was about to fall apart. The room was much brighter now due to the brightness of the lava that Scar created. The walls and the floors of the entire room were black, dark, and plain. A few chandeliers hung from the ceiling, many bright candles were attached to the ends, brightening the room a bit.

Scar's mallet fell right into her hand as she floated over to the stage. She looked around at the courtroom that she just created out of sheer will and lava and smiled brightly.

"We're almost ready folks! Sit sit! This is going to be the greatest trial of this century. I can feel it!" Scar gestured towards the empty seats, her cheerful yet intimidating demeanor not faltering for a second.

"This seems excessive..." Clay muttered to his sister, looking around at the court that had been created just to solve one simple argument.

Lucifer pushed past his children and sat at his throne. He didn't seem too worried about the situation. Sherry followed suit, standing next to his throne. Neither of them said a word.

Did they really need to conduct an entire trial for this? Almost everyone believed Nyx was back, except for Lucifer who was being overly stubborn, despite the answer being right in his face! Guess that's where Alyson got her stubborn nature from.

Satoru wasn't moving, he was just standing there with a concerned expression. His tail was wagging around slowly from side to side as if he was anticipating something bad to happen at any moment. He had to know what was going on. He worked with Scar after all.

Clay reached forward and lightly tapped Satoru on the shoulder. The Shadow Demon jumped slightly and turned to face him.

"What's going on? Can't you stop this or something?" Clay asked his friend, who just shook his head.

"I can't do anything to stop this. Scar is the demon in charge of all trials in Hell. It's not my position to stop her."

"But this is crazy! How does anyone trust Scar with carrying out justice?"

"Just, play along for now, and stay alive. I... I'll keep you safe. Okay? It's going to be okay," Satoru promised with a shaky breath. He didn't sound very confident in his words, but Claymore was honored, nonetheless.

Over the past few weeks of knowing Satoru in the flesh, Claymore had begun to trust him more and more. Though, he was starting to get a bit worried when Ally accused him of being a bad person. Thankfully he was able to push that aside when Sherry showed them all what happened on the day of the incident. Honestly, after seeing that, his relationship with Satoru felt like it strengthened.

"Mhm. Thank you, Satoru. I'm glad you're my friend." Clay smiled at him. Satoru's eyes widened ever so slightly, and he turned his head to face away.

"Oh? Pft, it's nothing. Don't worry about it!" Satoru gave Claymore a thumbs up and leaned against the free table where the two seats awaited Clay and Ally.

"Walk forward." Ally demanded.

"What? Why don't you go first?" Clay frowned.

"Because I don't trust this, and I got into a fight with Scar today. I would rather not start another one."

There was a loud crack on the center stage which caused them both to look up in surprise. Scar was smiling down at them, the small wooden table that had been on the stage previously, was now in tiny pieces across the entire stage. Her mallet was resting on her shoulder innocently, as if she didn't just destroy a table for the fun of it.

"Ahem! Since you're complaining, I've devised a new idea! I only need one of you to do all the chatting, so why don't one of you just sit there in silence? You don't have to be a part of this performance!" The Fire Demon announced.

Ally blinked and immediately ran to the chair on the right. "Perfect. Sorry Clay, you're better at arguing with logic than I am."

The second she sat down; the room went dark. A spotlight turned on above Clay, Ally, and Scar, causing Clay to close his eyes a little to avoid getting blinded. A drum solo began playing in the background. Clay felt himself tensing up.

"Ladies and gentlemen! Boys and girls! Welcome to the trial of the century, the Case of Nyx!" Scar put her hand to her face and blew a kiss towards the empty leather bench. When she blew it, flames came straight out of her mouth towards the bench. The flames floated around each of the seats and began to swirl around and take new forms. They were taking the forms of demons, but they weren't Fire Demons like Scar. They were just made of flames, nothing more. There were six of them in total watching Scar intently as she threw her mallet into the air above her.

Scar put her left hand on her chest, the other arm out like a warm invitation to join her on her stage. "Let us prepare and allow me to pass my judgment onto your demonic souls!"

The Fire Demon smirked, as red-hot chains crawled up from the floor, and quickly attached themselves to the back of Ally's chair. As they contacted her skin, it began to sizzle and smoke. Ally hissed in pain and immediately tried to get up, but the chains wrapped around her and pulled her back. Her hands sizzled as she continued to attempt to free herself. Clay could see marks being branded into her hands from the chains.

"Clay!" Ally screamed, as the chair held her in place. A chain was around her neck, burning into it slowly. She couldn't even try to free her neck, her hands were chained to the chair at this point, just like the rest of her. There were small tears of pain in her eyes, she looked panicked. The drum solo ended, and the room was silent for a second.

Clay turned towards Scar and slammed his fists on the table in front of him. "What the hell are you doing? Let my sister go!"

Scar just wiggled her finger at him. "I told you! She won't be a part of this trial! I don't see the issue!"

"You're hurting her!"

"Oh, she'll be alright if she stops trying to move! It's the water she should worry about!" Scar mused. Her mallet returned into her right hand, and she waltzed off her stage and stood in the middle of the room.

"Alright! Now that the extra has been contained, let us begin the trial!" Scar's tail pointed at Clay, and she clapped her hands with excitement.

Clay looked over at Satoru. Didn't he have some form of authority around her? Why was he letting this go on? His sister was being hurt right in front of him!

"Satoru, can't you make her stop? She's hurting my sister! Please, do something!" Clay pleaded with him, but Satoru just shook his head sadly.

"Again, I can't do anything, I'm sorry! She's the one in charge of the justice system in Hell, not me! Not even Sherry can stop her." Satoru whispered softly; his face was vacant of any expression at the time. "If Sherry doubted Scar's abilities, she wouldn't have allowed Scar to keep this position. Fair warning though, Scar does go a bit overboard with the theatrics."

"As per usual, I will explain the rules! Tell the truth and make it entertaining! I want a good show tonight, and I want it fast! Can't be late to the annual Halloween Gala! I got all dressed up after all!" Scar flipped her mallet around, so the hammer end was touching the ground and she could lean against the handle. "If you lose, or your argument starts to get boring, I will be forced to spice it up! By dropping our little extra right into the boiling water that's underneath her chair!"

Ally was silent in her chair. She wasn't bound by her mouth, so she could speak but she was too focused on the pain to try anything witty. Clay needed to get this over with and fast. He hated seeing his sister get hurt.

Clay looked under her chair. There was a trap door directly underneath it. He could hear water sloshing around underneath it. If she fell into the boiling water while being chained up, she'd get severely burned. Or worse...

"Most of the people here agree that Nyx has returned, except for Lucifer. I wouldn't be here if what I claim is a lie!" Clay announced, trying his best to sound confident. He could feel his palms sweating.

"Oh? And why's that?" Scar stared at Clay, not taking her eye off him. He wasn't a fan of the staring. Clay hated when people made eye contact with him like that. The spotlight from under Ally moved, so Clay was directly under the light again. He felt a lot more pressure on him. He had to stay focused and not let himself get overwhelmed.

"I just said why-"

"I heard you! I just want an explanation! Explain for the crowd, so we can hear your side! You want people to like you, no?"

Clay sighed, trying to think about the best way to handle this. He knew Scar wasn't to be trusted, but if she was in charge of the entire trial, he had to get on her good side somehow by telling the truth and entertaining. That's what she said to do.

"Satoru! He was at Aurora's house with me, my sister, and Lyly. He saw Nyx with his own eyes! You trust his judgment, right?" Clay said quickly, hoping that Scar would agree with him.

Scar was silent, her tail snapping at the air repeatedly. After a minute or so, she nodded and pointed at Satoru.

"Well, buddy o' pal! Is what Clay is saying true? Or is he a liar? Do tell!"

Satoru cleared his throat and nodded. "Mhm. He's telling the truth. I saw Nyx yesterday."

Sherry and Lucifer both stared at Satoru. Sherry didn't look fazed, while Lucifer just seemed angry that his point wasn't being the one proven right.

Scar giggled and clapped. "Well, share with the jury! What happened?" The spotlight now aimed at Satoru.

"Well, I think I'll have Claymore describe it. Since he had the best seat in the house. I was merely in his mind after all but, everything he's going to say, is true." Satoru said calmly, nudging Claymore lightly with his elbow.

The light now pointed directly at Clay as he raised an eyebrow at the demon boy's mischievous little smirk. Satoru was planning something. Hopefully it would help them end this trial as soon as possible.

"Excuse us for a moment, Scar. The performance will begin momentarily." Satoru put his elbows on the table and looked at Clay from the other side. He seemed to have calmed down.

"Here's what we'll do. I'll free your sister with my magic, while you tell Scar what happened yesterday. Make it fun. That way she'll be on our side," Satoru explained in a hushed sort of tone. "Try using your powers. She likes when people use visuals and stuff like that. Plus, I want to see what you can do. You might even surprise yourself!"

Clay nodded slowly, thinking about what he could do. He could make shadow ravens. That's really it. But his sister's life was on the line. He had to try harder and make this the most impressive telling of a horror story ever.

"I'll help you when I get the chance. I know you can do it Claymore." Satoru put a hand on Clay's cheek and gave him a reassuring smile, before walking around him, so he could stand behind Ally's chair.

"I can do this! I can do this..." Clay looked up at Scar, who was waiting expectantly. He looked at Ally and stood up onto the table. He had to keep everyone distracted, or Ally would potentially get dropped into boiling water.

"It was the evening, and we were about to set out towards Hell, to warn Lucifer," Clay paused to stare at Lucifer. He was barely paying any attention right now, which just made Clay want to punch the man. Nonetheless, he continued his explanation.

"Death- er, Aurora, had informed us that Nyx had been seen. She said that Nyx was planning on attempting to murder Lucifer at the Halloween Gala. So, we set out to try and warn him but just as we were about to leave, my sister forgot her blade in Aurora's house."

As he spoke, shadow creatures rose from behind Clay, towards the center of the room. The creatures formed around Scar, who was watching the show in amazement. The shadows twisted and changed, making a mini recreation of their encounter with Nyx at Aurora's. There was the kitchen and shadow versions of Clay and his sister, both unaware of what was about to happen. Was he making that happen? He wasn't even trying to!

"We found her knife. It was on the counter, but I felt something was wrong. I'm sure Satoru could too, he was in my mind at the time. But anyways, we went into the living room, and there it was. Nyx was sitting on the couch, staring at us with its singular red eye. It was terrifying." Clay continued, waving his hand from left to right.

He closed his eyes, trying to imagine something else to add to the miniature scene happening in front of him. He really hoped it would work and not blow up in his face.

When he opened his eyes, he was surprised to see that the image changed. There was a mini-Satoru on the set as well, standing behind Clay, looking nervous. The shadow versions were acting out the entire scene as he told the story. Clay felt impressed with himself. He didn't think he could make something as beautiful and terrifying as this with just some shadows and his own thoughts.

Lucifer leaned forward in his seat and stared at the shadows. Was Clay getting through to him somehow? Sherry didn't have a reaction, but he wasn't worried about her opinion. On the opposite side of the courtroom, Scar looked like she was thoroughly enjoying this entire production.

"Bravo! Bravo! Absolutely mind shattering!" Scar clapped and cheered, picking up her mallet and spinning around happily. "I believe this trial is kicking off quite smoothly! Oh, what fun!"

Clay looked back at his sister to check on her. She wasn't chained up anymore. The poor girl had marks all over her skin from the chains, burned into her flesh. She wasn't crying anymore, she looked furious. Satoru was standing beside her, shadow hands holding the broken chains in the air.

In the blink of an eye, Ally lunged at Lucifer, sitting at the table in front of her. She was holding her semi chewed knife in front of his face with her right hand, and a ball of flames in her left. "You! Listen to what my brother is saying, or I'll kill you before Nyx gets the chance to!"

"Ooh, what a turn of events! Even I didn't see that coming! Someone make some popcorn!" Scar cackled, hopping into the air and hovering there, watching the chaos unfold.

Clay didn't bother to stop Ally. He didn't really care if his father got injured. Lucifer allowed Ally to get hurt in the first place after all. Satoru stood next to Clay, his tail patting Clay gently on the head. Clay didn't mind whenever Satoru did that. It felt comforting.

"You did a great job back there," Satoru said softly, watching as Ally continued to threaten the King of Hell.

"It was thanks to you but, thank you anyways," Clay smirked.

Sherry was finally trying to do something. She was attempting to force Ally and Lucifer apart, but neither of them was listening. Lucifer had his hand raised, flames appearing in his hand. The ball of flames was growing larger by the second. Was he going to blow up the entire room? He was crazy!

"How dare you speak to me that way! I am your father!" Lucifer growled.

Ally spat in his face. "Boo hoo! I don't care! You're nothing to me!"

They both prepared to strike but before they could, something caused them both to freeze and stare at the middle of the room. The demons that Scar created disappeared with a shriek, shriveling away into nothing. Scar herself was just smiling with pure joy, like this was the best thing to ever happen to her.

In the middle of the room, stood Aurora. Slightly bruised up, and with her right arm in a black sling, but alive.

Her wardrobe was different from the last time Clay saw her. She had a black reaper robe on, with a dark blue trim. Patterns of skulls and bones were at the bottom of the robe. She didn't have the robe fully closed. Clay could see that she was wearing a neat Victorian styled suit, with a gray tie. Her hair was up in a small bun, with blue sapphires in her hair and a black rose in it that sat there proudly. It was quite beautiful.

Clay was so happy to see that she was alive, that he forgot all about Ally and Lucifer fighting. He had tried not to think about it, but he was scared that Nyx had killed her. Was it even possible for Death to die?

"I see I interrupted something of great importance." Aurora said sarcastically. She didn't have her scythe with her now. Hopefully it didn't get broken or lost in the fight with Nyx at the house.

"Miss Thunderstone! You're here early!" Lucifer immediately made his fire go out. Ignoring Ally, he got up from his throne, rushing over to greet Aurora.

He bowed slightly to her, smiling nervously. Aurora grabbed Lucifer by his ear and tugged on it hard. Lucifer yelped in pain, nearly falling forward from the shock.

"O-ow! The hell was that for? What did I do?" Lucifer complained.

Ally put her flames away as well, looking surprised by Aurora's sudden outburst towards the devil.

"I was fighting Nyx before I got here. I sent your children and their friends to warn you. And did you listen?" Aurora glared daggers at Lucifer, who shook his head.

"I- no. They're kids, why would I listen to them? I've never even met them before today! And besides, I don't want to think about the possibility of Nyx returning and trying to kill me!"

"Well, consider this a wakeup call because that's your reality. Nyx is going to try and kill you at the Gala, and you're not even prepared for a fight, are you?" Aurora tugged on his ear a little harder, and Lucifer yelped again.

"Alright alright fine! I'll play along! Just let go of me, will ya?" Lucifer pleaded.

Aurora hesitantly let him go and rolled her eyes. Seeing her like this was so different but Clay didn't mind at all. Someone had to knock some sense into Lucifer. Who better than Death herself?

"I can't cancel the party! Everyone is expecting it!" Lucifer yelled, taking a few steps back from Aurora, in case she tried to attack him again.

Sherry walked up behind him and coughed to get his attention. "If I may, sir, you can still have the party, if you're careful enough. Though, if you want to do this, everyone needs to get ready now. The Gala starts in less than an hour and most of you aren't ready."

Aurora nodded. "I agree with Sherry. Since you're being selfish, the Gala can continue but we must prepare for the eventuality of Nyx's attack during it. We'll have to think of ways to get the guests out of harm's way quickly and how to attack effectively. Can you do that in less than an hour, Lucifer?"

"Of course, yes. We have emergency training protocols for these situations. I'll have Sherry inform the guards…" Lucifer sighed and rubbed his ear.

Scar looked at everyone and clapped again. "Well, this trial is over with! I'll clean up, while everyone else gets ready for the Gala! The kids win! Huzzah!"

Clay grimaced, but he was glad the "trial" was over with. Now all he had to worry about was a Nyx attack. Great.

"Come on Clay. I'll show you the fitting room. I'm sure there will be something for you to wear there. You too, Ally." Satoru beckoned for them to follow which, they gladly did.

They didn't even get two feet out of the room before a group of maids and butlers approached them and whisked them all away to get prepared for the party.

CHAPTER ELEVEN

The Gala

"Ow! Cut that out! It hurts!" Ally snapped at the castle maid, as she forced a brush through her hair. She had been taken to a fitting room and told to sit down in a spinning chair with a mirror in front of it, where one of the castle maids was attempting to get her ready for the Gala. She wasn't big on parties or looking fancy, so this was a complete nightmare for her.

The maid had made her put on a suit for the party, as Ally was more comfortable with a suit, versus a dress. It was a black tuxedo with a white buttoned up undershirt and a black bowtie. The maid had put some yellow glitter around her eyes, similar to what Scar had on. She also put this weird black stuff under her eyes. Eyeliner, that's what the maid called it, but she made it look like wings near her eyes. It honestly looked really pretty.

"Hold still, miss!" The maid said worryingly at Ally, trying to finish fixing her hair. She looked like the type of demon Satoru was with light gray skin, black hair, and various burns and patches on her skin.

"This is stupid! I don't want my hair to look fancy!" Ally complained.

"It's not fancy dear! I'm just trying to brush it out! When was the last time you used a comb?" The maid sounded very concerned. Ally didn't see what the big deal was. She had better things to do than to brush out her hair constantly.

"My hair is fine! It's not that bad!" Ally hissed. The maid ignored her completely.

"Anyways, don't move or I'm going to accidentally burn you!" The maid said with a lot of enthusiasm. Ally felt the back of her hair being burned with a straightener.

"Your white-haired friend behaved better than you did, princess." The maid continued speaking to Ally and yanked the brush out of her hair, spinning her around to face the mirror. Her hair was brushed out completely and straightened. Nobody had done Ally's hair in a long time. It was kind of shocking to see it so neat after it being messy for so long.

"White haired friend? You mean, Lyly? Is she okay?" Ally asked slowly, feeling herself starting to zone out.

"Oh yes! She's been out of the hospital wing for a while now!" The maid said calmly.

Ally immediately wanted to see Lyly. She had been told that Lyly didn't die from the fire incident, which was a relief but the guilt from that event still had Ally in a chokehold. The moment that Ally found out that Lyly was alright, she wanted to apologize. Now she actually had the time to. All she had to do was find her.

"Do you happen to know where Lyly went?" Ally asked, glancing at the door behind her.

The maid chuckled and with enthusiasm said, "She was asking the same thing about you earlier. I can go get her if you'd like."

"Mhm, please do." Ally nodded.

The maid bowed slightly and exited the fitting room leaving Ally by herself.

Ally took this time to get out of her chair. Her entire body ached from being burned by those chains. The maid had to wrap Ally's skin up temporarily until the burns healed which according to the maid, wouldn't take that long. A few weeks at most.

The bandages weren't mostly visible due to her outfit but almost her whole body was covered with bandages, besides her face and head. The bandages around her neck itched and Ally worried that if she spoke too much, they'd come loose or break off somehow.

Her bookbag was on the ground which contained her books and her chewed up knife. She thought the books would help her, but she was wrong. Reading about demons was very different than being face to face with them. And the knife? Barely useful but it made Ally feel better by keeping it on her. She could use her fire abilities to an extent, but what if she couldn't when it mattered? She'd be defenseless without that battered up knife. So, Ally reached down and went through her bookbag, grabbing the knife and slipping it into her back pocket.

She had been able to use her fire abilities during the trial. It felt good to have that kind of power. Ally hoped that she had more chances like that to show off her abilities when Nyx showed up so she could prove it to herself. Though she had to make sure that she didn't touch Nyx, or she'd be done for.

"Yeah, I'll show them all. I'm not that bad at using these powers. Better than Claymore at least!" Ally whispered to herself, becoming her own hype man for a moment.

She looked at herself in the mirror once again amused about her appearance. As she stared into the mirror, she could see the door behind her open. A familiar white haired Humai was peeking her head into the room.

"Ally? The maid lady said that you were looking for me?" Lyly's ears twitched, and she opened the door, stepping inside the room.

Lyly was dressed for the Gala. Her hair had been cut slightly, so it was barely to her knees now. The top of her hair looked like it was in little twin buns, but the buns looked more like bows. Ally didn't really know much about hair terms.

Lyly was wearing an elegant looking white dress that went down to her kneecaps. It had white swirling patterns in the design and short sleeves. Ally had never seen Lyly in a formal dress, so it was a bit of a surprise. Lyly had on long light blue and white striped leg warmers that covered the rest of her legs, with white sneakers that gave her an extra inch or two of height. The heels on each shoe had a wing design. Just like Ally and Scar, Lyly had glitter around her eyes. Hers were a combination of dark and light blue. Lyly's necklace was on as well, it went nicely with her outfit.

Lyly looked so excited to see Ally again. Ally could see her tail wagging from side to side. "You look so cool!"

"Yeah uh, you too?" Ally said awkwardly. She still felt bad about the fire incident. She wanted to say something about it, but Lyly looked so happy right now. Then again Lyly was always cheerful. So, might as well pull off the bandage now while Ally still had the courage to.

"Listen, about earlier. I'm sorry for not listening to you. You got hurt because of me and I thought you were going to die." Ally stammered. "Even though Sherry said you'd be fine, I just felt so bad and-" Her words were coming out so fast that she couldn't even control what she was saying.

Lyly, being the considerate individual that she was, nodded in understanding. "It's okay. I survived, and you did too! That's what matters,"

"Yeah but, you could have been killed because I couldn't contain my own anger!"

"But I wasn't! It's alright Ally! Really! If anything, you're the one that you should be worried about," Lyly sighed softly. She could see the bandages wrapped around her neck. "How did that happen? Was that all from when you were fighting Scar?"

Ally shook her head. "No, it was from a trial that Scar held with us against Lucifer. I'm fine."

"But are you really? Ally, you're half demon but you're also half human. You can get hurt by things that hurt both species! You have to be careful too!" Lyly's ears went down. "My situation is different. I can handle more damage than you can."

"Is it because you're a Humai?"

"Something like that…" Lyly waved dismissively, walking towards the door. "The party is starting right about now. We should get going."

Ally rolled her eyes and went in front of Lyly, holding the door shut. "I have a question."

Lyly looked a little confused, her ears flopping to the side. "Yeah? What is it?"

"You were at my house the day of the incident, weren't you? You were the neighbor's white dog?" Ally interrogated.

Lyly looked away and nodded. So that's what Lucifer meant by sending Lyly to watch over them. But that still didn't explain something else. Ally thought that Lyly was sixteen. But how could she have been watching over them as a baby? That didn't make any sense!

Before Ally could ask any more questions, Lyly opened the door in front of them and the two walked away towards the great hall, where the Gala was supposed to be starting very soon.

They didn't speak on the way there. Lyly just skipped and hummed to herself, while Ally was deep in thought. Nyx was going to show up at this Gala. Which meant that she'd have to face it again and actually fight this time. But what about Lyly? Ally had never seen Lyly harm anyone. Would she be able to do it?

"You're the prince! You can't introduce yourself to the people with a messy tie!" Ally heard Satoru's voice hiss from around the corner. They were just about to reach the great hall.

"I thought I had it on properly!" Clay complained.

Curious, Ally rounded the corner, Lyly right at her heels. The boys were standing in the middle of the hallway, Satoru was adjusting Clay's tie for him.

Satoru's suit looked more like a medieval type, with a dark green long waistcoat over a black suit, with black loafers. He had numerous expensive looking silver buttons on his suit, and he had his hair up in a long ponytail. He had green jade jewels in his hair scattered throughout. Ally noticed that he was wearing white gloves too.

Clay's outfit looked more modern and honestly boring compared to Satoru. Though Ally wasn't going to say that to his face. Anyways, Clay looked like he was working for the government. Black suit, with black dress pants and loafers, like Satoru had. Clay's dark red tie was in the process of being fixed. Clay had white gloves on, just like Satoru. Maybe they planned that, or Hell only has one type of glove.

Claymore glanced over at Ally and smiled a little. "You look amazing Ally! You too Lyly!"

"Mhm. You look uh, fancy." Ally replied, watching as Satoru finished fixing Clay's tie. When he backed up, the tie looked much better.

"So, is everybody ready?" Satoru's tail swished around and lightly patted Clay on the head.

"Ready as I'll ever be…" Ally grumbled.

And with that, the four of them entered the great hall. The room was huge, filled with so many demons that all looked just as fancy as Satoru and Scar did. None of the other demons had jewels on them though.

The entire room was covered with orange and purple lights, so the room glowed with color. The ground was covered with so much smoke that it was almost impossible to see the ground. People's movements made the smoke swirl around, nobody paid attention to it.

On the right side of the room were the food and drink tables. A couple guards were standing by what looked to be a punch bowl, but the contents were bubbling. In the middle of the room, demons were dancing to classic ball music and showing off their beautiful attire. At the center of the dancing mob was Scar herself, entertaining the crowd as she spun and twirled. Least someone was having fun.

There were a good chunk of demons hanging off to the side, talking in circles and holding glass cups filled with various beverages. Ally could see Lucifer and Aurora talking to some old looking demons. Boring.

Ally was amazed to see so many different demons at the Gala. There were some that she had never even read about before! But she had to stay focused on the mission. Sherry and Aurora had agreed that the kids needed to keep a low profile, they would watch over the party to make sure nothing bad happened and when Nyx arrives, be ready.

"Can we get some snacks? Pretty please?" Lyly squealed, looking at the candy dishes on the tables.

"No. You'll get tired, and won't be able to complete our mission," Sherry answered for them as she walked by, her face buried in a clipboard. She wore a white button up shirt, with a light brown jumper dress with buttons down the middle of the front. Her silver hair was up in a long ponytail. She had miniature brown diamonds on the suspender part of her outfit and to top it all off, she had on brown leather boots.

"You have your jobs. Just because it's a party, doesn't mean that you can put your guard down. Focus."

Ally flipped Sherry the bird, as she walked away. There wasn't any harm in getting a snack. Besides, they hadn't eaten all day. They could use some food, even if it was junk. Fighting on an empty stomach wouldn't be good.

"Ignore her Lyly. Come on, let's get some food." Ally hissed, marching over to the tables of food. She could hear the others following right behind her.

As they were walking, a boy and a girl approached them. The boy looked like he didn't want to be there, while the girl was calmer and more collected looking.

232

The girl had ebony brown skin and pearly white eyes. Her light gray hair was braided, but Ally could tell that her hair was very long. She had various scars on her face, along with a birthmark in the shape of a crescent moon. She wore a navy-blue romantic gothic dress with silver heels. She had some kind of animal features on her head, not a dog. Probably a wolf. Anyways, she had a tail as well, it wasn't moving a mile a minute like Lyly's usually did. This girl seemed more mature and chill than Lyly was.

The boy next to her looked grumpy, like he was forced to make an appearance here. This guy had pale white skin that looked like he had never seen the sun in his life. His mouth was closed, but she could faintly see a pair of pointy fangs on either side of his mouth. He had dark brown hair that went down to the middle of his back, like Ally's did. His hair was wild looking, sticking up at weird angles. He had wine red eyes that matched his outfit, which was a dark red suit, with black sleeves, and black pants, along with black boots.

"Hello. Greetings from Valeria." The girl bowed slightly.

The boy mumbled something in a similar fashion, but he didn't bow. The girl smacked him on the back, then he bowed halfway.

Ally had no clue who these people were, or what they wanted from her. "Yeah uh, I have no clue who you are-"

The girl's ears twitched, and she nodded. "That's understandable. I've never seen you at these parties or any meetings...Parties are fun, they always have lots of new food to try..." Her voice trailed off.

Ally blinked and looked at Lyly. She wasn't sure what to make of this. Lyly didn't look like she knew what was going on either, so she just shrugged.

The boy waved his hand in front of the girl's face, which caused her to snap back to reality.

"Oh, thank you Nico... Anyways, where was I? Oh yes, we're from one of the kingdoms that's allied with your father." The girl exclaimed.

"How do you know who my dad is?" Ally stared at the girl.

"Your hair. You have that red streak. So does that other boy over there. I was just being observant..." The girl sighed. Her voice was low and very hard to hear. It sounded like she was whispering anytime she spoke.

"Nova, you're getting off subject again," Nico crossed his arms and huffed. As if he had anywhere better to be.

"Sorry. I tend to do that. At any rate, since we're the children of the people in charge of Valeria, I thought it would be good to say a friendly hello. That sort of thing." Nova's eyes darted towards the food table as she spoke. She sounded like she was losing any interest in the conversation that she started.

"Oh yeah? Well, he doesn't look very friendly to me." Ally stared at Nico, who glared in return.

Nova looked over at Nico and shot him a disappointed glare for a moment, before returning her attention to the table of food. "Mmm... He's usually like that. Father has me do the introductions, since I'm the oldest. But Nico has to come along anyways."

Ally could hear an entirely different conversation happening behind her. She really didn't care about what Nico and Nova had to say, so she turned around to eavesdrop on Clay's conversation. Lyly was starting up conversation with Nico and Nova instead.

Satoru was holding a plate of miniature sandwiches with his tail, while holding a cup of punch in his hand. Clay was talking to a couple of girls wearing fancy outfits.

They looked like they were around his age, and they seemed sweet enough. Both of them looked like Fire Demons.

"I'm sorry, I don't want to accidentally trip you and ruin your outfits," Clay fidgeted with his hands.

"Aw, it's okay! I didn't know the prince of Hell would be so sweet!" One of the girls squealed, her tail swishing around.

Satoru sipped his punch and rolled his eyes. "You know, you can't just stand around the whole time, Claymore. It's a party, everyone dances."

Clay glanced at Satoru. "I would if I knew how. I'd just make a fool of myself, and whoever I'm dancing with."

"You're a prince now, you have to know how to dance!" Satoru chuckled and set down his food on the table. "Come on, let's go."

"What?"

"I'm going to teach you your princely duties. Starting with, knowing how to dance!" Satoru grabbed Clay's wrist with his tail, and the pair walked off where the crowd of demons were dancing.

The two demon girls sighed and walked off to pester somebody else. Ally really hoped that nobody asked her to dance.

She wasn't a dancer, and she knew that she wouldn't be polite about it like Clay.

"Well, we should be going now. It was nice to meet you." Nova said softly, causing Ally to turn her attention back to the newcomers.

"It was nice to meet you both!" Lyly smiled and waved. Nova took Satoru's plate of food before walking off.

Nico stared at Ally, cursed at her under his breath, and walked off after his sister. Ally was in disbelief. She didn't have anything to say. Her mind was just blank. The audacity of that boy!

"They seemed nice!" Lyly beamed, her tail wagging.

Ally shrugged, watching Satoru and Clay. Satoru looked like he was having a great time leading Clay around. Clay's expression was comedy gold. He looked so nervous and kept almost stepping on Satoru's feet, but Satoru didn't pay any mind to that. His tail was wagging and catching Clay whenever he was almost to stumble backwards. It was honestly really sweet.

"Well, well well! Look who's here! Alyson Siberia!" A voice cackled next to Ally.

Ally shuttered as she felt Scar poking the side of her head. She didn't even want to look at that demon. Not after their fight. Ally still wasn't over that.

"Go away, please…" Ally whispered faintly.

Scar just laughed and stood in front of Ally. Scar had that stupid smile on her face. If Ally wasn't so afraid right now, she'd smack it off.

"Aw, is somebody scared? I can make all those fears go away!" Scar grabbed a spoon from the food table and bit the top half off. "If you let me possess you, you won't be afraid anymore! Come on, my offer isn't going away anytime soon!"

"I already told you. Forget about it." Ally stared at the ground; her hands were trembling.

Lyly's ears went down, and her expression changed into one that Ally rarely saw from her. Anger.

"Ally already told you no. So, get lost!" Lyly commanded.

Both Scar and Ally were stunned into silence. Lyly's voice was so firm. That usual hint of sweetness in her voice was gone, replaced by whatever was fueling her rage now.

"Oh? You again? I thought you were knocked out from that smoke. What happened to that?" Scar mused, patting Lyly on the head a few times.

Lyly shook her head and snapped at Scar's hand, nearly biting it. Now Ally was shocked. Violence, coming from Lyly? Was Ally dreaming right now?

Scar pulled her hand back quickly and giggled. "Aha! Nice try! But you'll have to be faster than that to catch me!"

"Bother Ally again, and I won't miss next time." Lyly glared at the Fire Demon, who just smiled as per usual.

Scar glanced around seeing Sherry wandering around with her clipboard again. "Alright, fine. But I'll be back! Just you wait…" And with that, Scar was off to annoy Sherry. Ally watched as Scar floated above Sherry, probably asking a million questions or something like that, as she munched on that metal spoon.

Ally looked at Lyly in amazement. "Lyly I- thank you…"

Lyly's ears stuck back up, and her face returned to the happy expression Ally was used to seeing. "Aw, don't mention it! That's what friends do!"

Lyly was right. They really were friends now, huh. It was strange to think about, but they were. After all those years of Ally hating her guts, Lyly had managed to befriend her.

"Everyone, gather round! I have a little announcement to make, before this Gala progresses any further!" Lucifer's voice echoed around the entire great hall.

Everyone turned to Lucifer as he stood in the center of the room. His attire was the same as it was earlier. Lazy ass.

Underneath him, a small platform began to rise, so he towered over all the other demons more than he usually did. He held a black cane with a red glowing star on it. The light coming off it was the same kind from when someone holds a flashlight underneath their chins.

"Now I know this is a bit early. But next Spring, we will be hosting The Hell Games! Yes, they're coming back again!" Lucifer exclaimed into his cane. It made his voice louder like a microphone.

The other demons clapped and cheered respectfully. Lucifer smiled and bowed, clearly enjoying everyone's praise. Ally just rolled her eyes. Lucifer didn't look worried at all. He really didn't believe that his life was in danger. What a moron.

Lyly's ears stuck up as she stared at Lucifer. Her expression changed to a look of worry and panic. "Ally, we need to move."

Ally scoffed. "Yeah, we've been standing in the same spot for this entire party. Maybe I could try my luck at dancing without making a fool of myself."

"No, that's not what I mean!"

"Well, what do you mean then?"

Ally tensed up. She realized something was wrong, in fact she could hear something cracking loudly behind her. Without hesitating for a second, Ally and Lyly ran forward at the same time, as the wall behind them crumbled, and bits of rubble were flying all around them.

Ally could hear the screaming of the partygoers ahead. Sherry barked some orders to Lucifer. It was utter chaos within seconds.

Sadly, Ally hadn't started running in time to fully evade the falling wall. A large chunk of stone crushed the food table, bits of the table leaning towards Ally and Lyly. A large portion of the table tumbled forward and caught Lyly by her tail, causing Lyly to fall.

Ally turned around to see it happen. There was something crawling out from the broken wall, but she wasn't focusing on that. Lyly was stuck.

It was a repeat of the fire incident. Ally was caught up in her emotions, but this time was different. She was aware of what was happening to her friend now, and she couldn't just stand by.

"Ally! You need to run!" Lyly squeaked, trying to pull herself free.

Ally marched over to Lyly and grabbed her, trying her best to help free Lyly. "Shut up! I'm not leaving you to die!"

After a few tugs, Lyly was free. A couple pieces of hair from her tail had been ripped out, but Lyly didn't complain. At least she was safe now.

Ally looked at the hole in the wall, squinting her eyes to look at what was crawling in. It was hard to see. "Alright, now let's deal with-" She stopped. She recognized what was appearing.

A mass of black tentacles and hair crawled into the room, blood dripping from bits of the goo all over its body. Its blood red eye staring into Ally's soul, as it grabbed its head, and tilted it so it was facing her perfectly.

It was smiling at her behind the layers of goo. The black wings behind Nyx were slowly rising, as two large tentacles lurched forward.

There were bodies attached to the tentacles and Ally knew who they were from the moment she saw them. On the left, the body of a woman with light brown hair who had amber yellow eyes except the eyes were no longer there but replaced by a black void, and a tentacle going through the back of her head, puppeteering her. On the right, a little boy at the age of eight with his head spun the opposite direction. His legs were bent at an angle as if he had fallen recently. His eyes had also been removed from their sockets. What was left of them was probably melted into the goo all around him. Ally could see his red streak of hair underneath the goo, it was the only bright thing about him now.

Her heart felt like it had stopped. Demons around her screamed, rushing to get out of there. Ally could still hear the music being played from somewhere nearby.

"Mom! Elliot!" Clay screamed from the dance floor. Ally could see him out of the corner of her eye. Satoru was standing in front of him, looking ready for a fight. Shadow hands had already appeared beside him. Nyx stared directly at Ally and crawled forward towards her at record speed.

Everything happened so fast. Ally barely had time to react but in the nick of time, Ally jumped back, as she made balls of fire with her shaking hands and threw them into Nyx's face.

Nyx landed just mere inches away from Ally, the goo dripping on the floor behind it. Its face was being burned by the flames, the bodies of her family were swinging around bashing into tables and walls being destructive.

This was it. Nyx was here and Ally wasn't going to let it win without a fight.

CHAPTER TWELVE

Nyx's Corpse Puppets

Clay was panicking, he couldn't get to Nyx just yet. Satoru was standing in the way preventing him from joining the fight. Clay's breath was shaky, and his heart felt like it was going to explode out of his chest.

He wasn't expecting to see his dead mother and brother's corpses at the party. What did Nyx do to them? Why? What would it need with them? How twisted in the head was Nyx, that it decided to do that?

"Satoru, let me help!" Clay snapped, his whole body shaking with rage. He wanted to tear Nyx apart and make it feel the same pain that his mother and brother felt that day and then do it all over again, just for good measure.

Satoru looked very hesitant to allow Clay to fight. He glanced at Nyx, then back at Claymore. "Okay but, I'm sticking with you." Satoru nodded.

Clay sighed and waved his hand, making a shadow raven appear that flew around Clay's head. "I won't stop you! Just let me attack that thing!"

"Understood. Come on." Satoru ran forward with Clay closely behind. The various shadow creatures that had been created followed both Satoru and Clay.

Before they could get close enough to attack Nyx, the tentacles holding Elliot's corpse lunged right at them, stopping them progressing any further. Clay didn't have any time to cry, he knew that his brother was dead but seeing Nyx mutilate his body was too much. He wanted vengeance.

"Attack." Clay growled.

Satoru's tail stood up in alarm. "But that's your brother!"

"Not anymore. My brother is dead. That is a monster. I don't want it to hurt anyone." And with that, Clay charged. The shadow raven flying ahead of him, flying around Elliot's corpse, searching for a weakness of sorts.

Clay didn't see one himself and he knew that he couldn't get much closer or he might get accidentally corrupted.

Clay waved his hand again as he ran to the side, trying to get around Elliot's corpse but it kept getting in the way at every turn, doing whatever it took to keep Clay away from his sister.

"Is there a weakness to this stuff?" Clay yelled out to Satoru, who was fighting off a smaller tentacle with his shadow hands nearby.

"We never figured that out!" Satoru yelled back.

"That's not very helpful!"

"I know- look out!"

Clay spun around just in time to see a table flying at him, and then he was thrown across the room. He landed against the wall and immediately tried to get up. His whole body was aching, but there was no time to rest.

He looked over at his sister and he was surprised to see that she was standing her ground very well so far. She was continually backing up while hurling balls of flames at Nyx's face, while managing to stay clear of any attacks Nyx tried to throw at her. Lyly was quickly running around picking up random pieces of rubble and tossing them at the gooey tentacles.

Satoru was fighting Elliot's corpse, but where was his mother's? Clay glanced behind him, hoping she wasn't there. To his relief, she wasn't, but that feeling of relief quickly turned into sheer panic as he saw his mother's body dangling behind Ally reaching towards her with a gooey hand.

"Ally!" Clay stood up racing to Ally with his hand held out in front of him. Could he make another bird? No, that wouldn't work. A raven could only do so much. Think, think, think! He felt himself slipping forward, everything was in slow motion as he watched his mother's corpse about to attack. He knew that he wouldn't be able to reach her on foot in time.

"Ally…" He whispered weakly to himself. He couldn't lose her. Not now. Not when they were so close to finishing this nightmare. He'd be all alone. Sure, he had friends like Lyly and Satoru, but Ally had been with him for pretty much his entire life. She was his little sister, the only family that he had left. As he thought, his mind began to wander to a simpler time.

The earliest memory he had was sitting on the couch with his baby siblings. The windows were open, a cool breeze was flowing through the living room. His mother, Cora was doing laundry and other household chores and had set Elliot and Ally down while she worked…

He closed his eyes, falling into his own thoughts as the world around him faded into black.

"Clu-a-more!" Young Clay smiled patiently at his siblings, trying to get them to say his full name. They hadn't been able to just yet. Mom told him that it might be too long or too difficult to understand for a two-year-old but that didn't stop him from trying.

"Clay!" Young Ally giggled. She was able to pronounce the shortened version of his name just fine. She did try to say the full one but every time she'd just throw a tantrum when Clay tried to encourage her.

"Bubba!" Elliot clapped and began to giggle alongside his sister. Oh, how much Clay would pay to hear him call him that again.

Young Clay sighed and held his hands together, keeping his gentle smile. "So close! You'll get it someday! It's a big word, but I believe in both of you!"

Elliot and Young Ally's eyes lit up, and they both leaped forward, trapping Young Clay in a hug. Young Clay just laughed and embraced them.

Why couldn't things stay that way? Why did life have to be so cruel? Did he do something to deserve this?

To deserve watching his family get torn apart right before his very own eyes. To helplessly watch his little sister, get into one bad situation after the next?

He was useless during the incident. Alyson could have died that day. The only reason she lived was because of Satoru. Another time was when Sherry and her pet snake were chasing them. Clay couldn't do anything as Ally got bit and was motionless on the ground at his feet. He couldn't stop Scar from trapping her in a circle of fire and beating her up. And when Scar had her in those chains with her skin burning, she had been crying in pain. Claymore couldn't do much to help her then either. Utterly useless.

He didn't deserve to have Ally as his sister. The sister that stuck by his side for all these years. The same sister that dragged him around and always went out of her way to talk to him even when she was in a bad mood.

Clay opened his eyes. He could feel tears forming, but he didn't care. It wasn't going to end like this. He wasn't losing Ally too. He was her big brother and he had to protect her.

As he started to fall to the ground, there was a loud sudden bang next to him. The sound rang in his ears, it was an awful feeling.

His hearing would surely get messed up from that experience. He had no clue what happened. Did someone shoot a gun? That's what it reminded him of.

Lyly paused as she was mid throw to look at Clay. "Wow, I didn't know you could do that! That's pretty cool!"

What was she talking about? He looked at his hand that was extended and to his surprise, he was holding a revolver made from shadows. The barrel had a faint trail of smoke coming out of it. He wasn't even trying to create a gun. He didn't think he was able to create more than just ravens.

Clay looked at the body of his mother. There was black goo pouring out of her eye sockets and dripping all over the floor. His mom's body wasn't trying to attack Ally anymore. It looked weary. Hesitant? It was a corpse being controlled by Nyx. The body couldn't feel any emotions.

Meanwhile, Ally took this chance to pull her knife out from her back pocket and slash at the creature, causing it to back away from her, as it was clearly wounded.

"Whatever you just did, keep doing it Claymore!" Ally shouted; her eyes fixed on the "Cora" monster.

"Right!" Clay quickly got up and ran to Ally, standing behind her and facing the opposite direction. He held the shadow revolver tightly firing it at Nyx to keep it at bay. Nyx kept trying to get back near Ally, but Clay wouldn't let it. They were both keeping the two corrupted beings away once they got the hang of it. Shoot. Stab. Dodge. Repeat. It felt so natural to Clay even though he had never fought like this before.

"I was right about this evening! I knew it would be entertaining!" Clay heard Scar's voice cheer from behind him followed by a loud crunch and a shrill of laughter.

He glanced behind him quickly and was surprised to see Scar standing right in the middle of all the action, holding her mallet proudly then throw it in the air while her other hand was held out held behind her shielding Satoru and Lyly. Scar had a murderous look in her eye with bits of lava dripping from her teeth. This was the only time Clay had ever been grateful for Scar's presence.

Satoru and Lyly were standing behind her. A hole was in the ground nearby. It looked like the size of Scar's mallet. Lyly was holding pieces of trash. Clay wasn't sure why.

Satoru was frozen in fear. Elliot's corpse was swinging around in the air in front of Scar, but the Fire Demon didn't look afraid in the slightest.

Scar dipped her head backwards violently so she could stare at Lyly and Satoru. Her neck should not have been able to do that. "Everyone knows that the kiddos aren't as skilled as I in the art of battle. Allow me to educate you two!"

Scar raised her mallet into the air and threw it once again. She began doing a similar dance to the one that she did to create the courtroom, but this one was a bit different. Instead of flicking her wrists to create lava, she slowly spun around with her eye closed. She looked content with what she was doing. As Scar spun around, flames spawned from her claws and flowed around her, preventing Elliot's corpse from attacking all of them for the time being.

"Ah, I miss moments like this! It really makes me feel like I'm on stage!" Scar smiled, her fangs shining with the lights of the flames.

"Scar, look out!" Lyly yelped.

The Elliot corpse seemed to have enough of Scar's nonsense. He came swinging through the flames, ready to smash Scar, Satoru, and Lyly into little bits.

Elliot's corpse didn't have a chance. Scar suddenly stopped her dance, staring the corpse down.

The flames around Scar froze in midair and with a shrill squeal of delight, her tail snapped in the air causing the flames to move once more and attack Elliot with all of her strength. The flames engulfed Elliot's corpse burning what was visible of the body. Scar's mallet came flying back out from the sky, smacking Elliot's corpse in the face. Next thing Clay knew, Elliot's corrupted form was laying on the ground smoking with Scar's mallet left undamaged next to him.

Satoru made his shadow hands poke Elliot's corpse. It was not getting back up. One down, two more to take care of.

So, the puppets could be defeated even though their bodies were dead and covered with corruption goo, Elliot and Cora were mere humans. Human bodies could only withstand so much before breaking down, even dead ones. That gave Clay an idea.

"Ally! Aim for mom!" He shouted to Ally, as Lyly threw a piece of trash at Elliot. Once again, he didn't move.

Ally didn't look at him, but she nodded in understanding and started lunging at their mother's body, slashing at the face with her knife and anything else she could reach without getting too close. Clay had no clue why she wasn't using her fire powers, but at least she was fighting.

He waved his hand, and a shadow shotgun appeared above him and he fired it at Nyx. Nyx screeched as it was blown backwards by the shadow bullets. Clay's ears were still ringing, and he couldn't hear anything but that wasn't important right now.

He aimed his revolver at the Cora corpse and fired. His finger was feeling numb from the number of times he was pulling the trigger. He would have felt bad if that was his mom, but he knew that she was gone. This was just a monster of what remained.

Cora's body jerked as the shadow bullets hit it over and over. It kept trying to reach for Ally, but Clay wouldn't let her near Ally. He continued to shoot off his revolver until Cora's body fell to the ground in a heap.

"Is she done?" Lyly called from across the room somewhere, putting down the trash in her arms and walking over to Clay.

"I think so…" Clay nodded, his shadow revolver disappearing. He was proud of himself for once. He was able to create something to keep Ally and himself safe. He was finally enough.

"Seems Nyx is running off! A coward, that creature!" Scar cheered. Satoru chuckled a bit even Ally couldn't help but smirk at that comment.

Clay stayed silent looking over at Satoru. Satoru didn't look injured, just winded. Thank goodness.

As Lyly stood next to Clay, her ears stuck up. Her cheerful demeanor changed, switching to a look of panic.

"What?" Clay was starting to feel uneasy.

Lyly looked like she was about to say something but before she could, a tentacle reached forward in front of Claymore. It was so fast that Clay didn't have time to react. Nyx crawled out from wherever it was flung earlier, grinning like mad. It was over. Clay lost. He was going to become Nyx's newest corpse puppet and join his family as another victim of Nyx.

He felt himself getting pushed to the side and suddenly he was on the ground. The gooey tentacle was wrapped around Lyly's head, holding her in the air. Her legs were kicking trying to get herself down. NO! NO!

The tentacle lifted Lyly higher and threw her across the entire great hall, her body smashing into all the light fixtures, causing them all to break and crash to the ground. The room got darker and darker as the lights burst. All he could see now was Lyly and the rest of his friends.

Clay couldn't bear to watch as he saw the first drops of blood spilled. He ran towards Lyly as her body crashed into the back wall and laid still there. He heard footsteps rushing behind him, it sounded like Ally.

"Don't touch her! S-she's going to become one of those monsters!" Satoru screamed, throwing his shadow hands around Clay to try and keep him from Nyx. Nyx was staring at Lyly, its eye wide and ears down as if in a trance. It was still picking up things and throwing them at Scar and Satoru with its gooey tentacles.

Clay struggled out of the shadow hands to make it to Lyly and knelt by her side. Ally was just standing in front of her, gripping her knife so tight that her palm was turning white. She just stared at Lyly in silence, not saying anything or doing much to help.

Lyly looked pretty beat up, cuts from the chandelier and new open wounds over her exposed skin. Her dress was torn, and her head had a nasty cut along the forehead, dripping blood down her entire face. She needed stitches badly. It made Clay feel queasy just to look at it. The strange thing about this was the fact that she didn't have any goo on her. Nyx had touched her and grabbed her head with a tentacle. Why wasn't Lyly corrupted? Did it take a long time to corrupt someone? This doesn't feel normal.

Scar didn't look very freaked out about the situation. She still had her usual grin. She was starting up her dance once more, ignoring everything that just happened, flames spinning around her.

Nyx growled and raised a twisted hand. A smaller tentacle shot out from its back and grabbed the remains of a table. Before anyone could react, Nyx threw the table at Satoru which sent him flying backwards. Another table was thrown, and it smacked Scar in the stomach, sending her back with Satoru. Clay saw Scar's eye shut. That was not good. They needed her strength! Satoru's tail was pinned down by the table and he looked too tired to use any more magic to free himself. He was desperately trying to use his actual hands to lift the table off his tail, but it wasn't working. They were so screwed.

Lyly's ears suddenly twitched, and she sat up, her eyes were fixed on Nyx. Her hands were balling into fists. There was no way she should be able to do any of that. Humai or not, no one could get up so fast and move around after being thrown like that unless Humai were really strong super humans or something.

"Don't worry, I'll protect you...you guys!" Lyly gritted her teeth, blood starting to pour slowly from her mouth. She was attempting to fully get up. Clay didn't know she was this determined to fight someone. It was like her, and Ally switched minds.

"Lyly, you can't fight, you need to rest!" Clay hissed, holding his arms out to catch Lyly. She looked like she was about to pass out, but she wasn't stopping.

Lyly's hair began to blow around despite there being no wind. She grabbed onto Clay and used him to help pull herself to her feet. Her legs were scratched and cut, her knees were wobbly, but she didn't stand down. Once she thought she could handle herself, she released her grip on Clay, putting her hands together. A high-pitched humming noise filled the room, causing the room to shake. Ally and Clay looked at each other, neither of them knew what was happening.

"Lyly! Sit down! Don't be an idiot, you're hurt!" Ally shouted at her, but Lyly didn't listen. She was tuning everyone out, her ears were down.

Satoru's voice could be heard from underneath a broken table. "Watch out above you! Move!"

Clay looked up. The chandelier above their heads was spinning around on the string in midair lowering towards them. The candles on it were already out. As it spun it was getting closer to their heads. Clay waved his hands. His shadow shotgun returned and fired at Nyx once more. The shot echoed across the room, causing the chandelier to break free from its bonds and fall exactly where they were all standing.

Lyly clapped her hands, right as Clay grabbed Ally and Lyly, pulling them back while the chandelier crashed down in front of them. The room shook from what Clay assumed was the force of the chandelier shattering, knocking them all backwards. Bits of glass and material scratched their skin and got into their hair. Clay felt something dripping down his left arm, and it wasn't just fresh blood. There was candle wax burning away at his skin on his arm. He shrieked in pain and shook his arm, flicking some wax off him. It hurt like hell.

Lyly was sitting on the ground with her head down, blood dripping down her mouth and staining her pretty dress. Her eyes were closed as she sat in a pool of her own blood. Clay could see that she was breathing. She'd be okay. But, how? She still didn't look corrupted. Was she immune somehow? Was that even possible?

Ally was laying close by, her right arm resting in the pool of Lyly's blood. Her eyes were closed too. Neither of them seemed to be conscious. Clay was the only one awake to defend them against Nyx.

"Ally! Lyly! Wake up!" Clay grabbed Ally by the wrist and shook her, attempting to wake her up to no avail. He didn't bother trying to wipe their collective blood off himself, even though it was gross.

"Five more minutes…" Ally mumbled and then went silent again.

"Ally! Get up!" He continued shaking her desperately. He glanced back at Lyly. To his surprise, the blood pool was swirling around and glowing white. It was the only source of light in the entire room now, showing exactly where they were for Nyx to attack.

He was too panicked to question why the blood was doing it or why Lyly's blood that got onto Ally and Clay was also glowing. They just needed to survive. Fight now and ask questions later.

"Al! We need to fight!" Clay screamed, which forced Ally to finally open her eyes. Her expression was very dazed and confused, until she remembered what happened moments ago.

Ally nodded, and stood up quickly, extending her hand to pull him up next to her. He took it, feeling like their luck was just starting to turn.

He let go of Ally's hand and turned to try and fight Nyx again but to his horror, Nyx was standing behind them, gooey tentacles extended out towards them. Before Clay or Ally could get away, Nyx grabbed them both, lifting them up by their arms.

It didn't say anything, it just stared at the two of them. Clay gulped. They were about to get corrupted too, weren't they? Probably right now!

Clay's arm stung. It felt like Nyx was going to pop it out of his socket. Why did it have to grab his left arm? Strangely, besides that, he didn't feel any different or corrupted. He looked over at his sister. She wasn't being corrupted either.

"Clay!" Ally called for his attention, as another tentacle rose from behind Nyx, twisting and turning into the form of a sword.

He knew what had to be done. The low lighting made it difficult to see where Nyx's face was and then just like that, his vision began to blur. It was just like before when he first saw Sherry in her true form as a demon. He wasn't scared nor freaked out like last time. He knew what to expect.

When his vision returned, he could see Nyx perfectly. Nyx's figure and Ally were the only white things he could see. The rest of the room was pitch black. It was much easier to just see Nyx now.

When he looked at Ally, her eyes were trained on Nyx. Was she able to do the same trick he was doing? It was possible, they were both demon kids after all. He never asked her about it, but he should after this is all done.

Clay waved his free hand, shadows twisting against their will into the shape of a large raven. It squawked and flew at Nyx's face immediately. The raven's claws scratched in the area that Nyx's face was supposed to be causing Nyx to yell out in pain and release Ally and Clay.

They landed on the ground, and both began to attack using their abilities as much as they could. Ally held out her hand and flames roared to life, attacking Nyx in the face as well.

Now that they knew they couldn't get corrupted, the fight got a lot more interesting. Not being able to make physical contact with Nyx was the difficult part before but now all they had to do was kill Nyx! How hard could that be? The Cora and Elliot corpse bodies went down quick. No matter what, Ally and Clay would figure it out and finish what Nyx started.

"On your right!" Clayed called out to Ally as a tentacle swished past Ally's right side. Thankfully she dodged out of the way just in time, giving him a quick nod of gratitude.

Clay stayed at a distance from Nyx, creating more creatures from shadows to launch at Nyx. He was getting the hang of making things with his powers, especially different types of weapons.

He had to be careful not to accidentally shoot his sister, as she was now getting up close and personal with Nyx. He didn't understand how she wasn't scared. Ally was so fast. It was hard to keep up with her attacks. One minute she'd be slashing at Nyx's tentacles with her beaten up knife, the next she's burning Nyx's face area with flames in her other hand.

Nyx was having trouble fighting back. It felt good to finally be able to attack the creature and go all out. It deserved it after all. Nyx was barely getting to attack back at this point. Clay and Ally must have caught it by surprise.

Clay didn't even register that he was starting to get hurt more. Nyx was desperately throwing bits of broken debris at Clay. They were small but were deadly enough to hurt him. He felt one hit his ribs, causing him to wheeze in pain and stumble, but luckily, he was able to regain his balance before suffering any greater injuries.

Nyx screeched in agony and a giant wall of goo appeared out of nowhere, separating Nyx from Ally and Clay. He couldn't see Nyx anymore. Where did it go?

"Clay! Ally!" Lyly coughed from her spot on the floor. She was starting to wake up.

Clay looked at Lyly and was horrified to see Nyx standing in front of Lyly. Not moving, just staring. Its wings flapped, its ears twitched up and down slightly. It reminded Clay of a curious dog, in a twisted sense.

"Leave her alone!" Ally screamed and charged at Nyx.

Before Ally could reach them, Nyx turned to face Ally, its grinning face burning its image into Clay's mind and just like that, Nyx melted into the floor, and was gone. His mom and brother's bodies melted away as well.

Ally stopped a few feet away from Lyly, staring at the spot on the floor where Nyx previously was. Ally's hand was shaking, blood sliding down her bandaged arms. Her breathing was really loud as she was coming down from the adrenaline rush. Clay was too. His bones ached. He wanted to crawl into bed and stay there forever. How did he not realize how much he was hurting until now? Rage does wonders for pain apparently.

From behind him, Clay heard a couple pairs of footsteps rushing into the room. His shadow creations disappeared, and his vision returned to normal as he sighed and turned around to face the great hall's entrance. Sherry and Lucifer arrived. Where the hell were they during this fight? Cowards.

"Oh. You're alive and not corrupted…" Sherry stared at them blankly, holding her silver spear. Lucifer was behind her, neither of them looked injured.

"Where were you during that fight? Huh?" Ally barked, sitting by Lyly's side, refusing to turn around.

"As the King of Hell, my life is more important than anyone else's here. I must be away from the fights," Lucifer responded coldly.

"We are your kids, you dead beat!"

"You're the ones that decided to fight. You could have gone to safety too, I suppose."

"Screw you!"

Sherry hit the end of her spear on the floor, causing Lucifer and Ally to stop their argument and pay attention to her instead. "Ahem! We have bigger matters to discuss such as where are Scar and Satoru?"

Clay's eyes widened. He forgot about them. Last time he saw them, they were both trapped by the table that Nyx threw at them. He hoped they were still there.

"Over here!" Satoru's hand stuck up from underneath a broken table. "We're fine! Just stuck!"

Sherry sighed and slowly made her way over to the table. It looked heavy. There's no way she'd be able to lift it by herself. Sherry didn't even set her spear down. She picked up the table with one hand, lifting it enough so Satoru could get out. Clay made a mental note to never mess with Sherry.

Satoru crawled out and pulled Scar out with him. She was beginning to return to consciousness.

Scar's eye opened slowly, and she immediately floated next to Sherry, a wide grin on her face as if everything was fine. "What a show! Absolutely wonderful performances!"

Satoru dusted himself off. He didn't look as happy as Scar did. "You two fought well. I'm still confused about what happened, but whatever you did, it worked."

Sherry set the table back down and took a deep breath. "None of the guests were injured. I was able to get everyone out in time. No casualties that I know of. Now, tell me what happened here."

Clay didn't know what to say. They fought Nyx and didn't die. That's what happened but probably not the response that Sherry was looking for.

"Me and Scar couldn't help with fighting Nyx much. It got the better of us, sorry boss," Satoru spoke up.

"It's fine. At least you're alive. Did you get to see what happened?" Sherry questioned.

Satoru glanced at Clay, then back at Sherry. "Well at first, Nyx was using Clay's mom and brother's corpses to attack people. Guess that explains why the bodies were gone from their house on the day of the incident. Scar was able to stop Elliot's body from attacking. Clay shot Cora's."

Lucifer shot a quick glare at Clay, then huffed. "What happened after that? And make it snappy. I'm in a bad mood."

Satoru nodded. "Yes sir… Nyx grabbed Lyly and threw her into the lights. Lyly's alive and she's somehow not corrupted! I thought I was hallucinating. That shouldn't have been possible, right?"

"Correct. That doesn't make any sense. I'll have to investigate it. Nobody's been immune before. Then again, we don't know that much about the corruption." Sherry's tail twitched.

"Ally and Clay went to check on her, and then Lyly tried attacking. I'm not sure what she was doing, it was hard to see because the lights went out. There was this humming noise, it really hurt my ears and then Nyx attacked. And um, fighting? I think? It really blurs together, and it was hard to see…" Satoru mumbled.

"Nyx grabbed me and Ally, but we didn't get corrupted. Also, Lyly's blood was glowing and swirling around. It was weird." Clay said quickly, hoping to help Satoru a bit. It was the least he could do after all.

"What? That doesn't make sense." Lucifer grumbled. Very helpful.

"Sir. Do you know what this means?" Sherry said slowly.

"…That the kids were right?'

269

"Well, yes, but that's not what I was talking about." Sherry sounded hopeful. "It means that your children are immune to corruption, somehow. They could banish Nyx without worrying about getting turned into a monster. That is, if they're up to the task."

"What's in it for us?" Ally got up from her spot near Lyly and walked over to Sherry.

"Revenge, I suppose. For all the souls Nyx killed and turned into monsters. You're not the only ones that have lost family members to Nyx. It's been doing things like this for centuries."

"Revenge sounds good... Clay, what do you think?" Ally looked at Clay for reassurance.

Clay nodded slowly. He wanted Nyx to pay for killing his mother and brother. Their souls would be avenged. "I'll do it if Satoru and Lyly can help us."

"We've got your back Clay!" Lyly smiled and coughed up more blood. She really needed to get some medical help.

"Of course I'll help." Satoru nodded as well, patting Clay on the head with his tail.

"Oh and, Aurora sends her regards. She had to leave for business or something..." Lucifer added.

That made Clay feel much better, as he only saw her at the party for a moment before Nyx arrived.

"If you're going to defeat Nyx, the other kingdoms need to be aware of this."

"Other kingdoms?" Clay wondered. There were other kingdoms now?

"Yes, there are other ones. You're lucky that I have alliances with most of them. I'll set up meetings and speak with their leaders. We all need to be on guard if and when Nyx attacks again."

"I met two kids from Valeria." Ally brought up.

Satoru chuckled. "Nico and Nova Ryder. They're the children of the rulers there. That's good that you've already been introduced. It'll make things easier."

Clay was shocked that Ally spoke to someone else without him being around. She was growing out of her shell. He was proud of her and it was great to witness.

"Now then. You all need to get fixed up. Let's all go to the infirmary, and work on plans later. There's still much left to learn." Sherry began to walk off, gesturing for everyone to follow her. Lucifer followed next to her, Scar following suit too.

Satoru waved his hand, and a shadow hand appeared, lifting Lyly up so she didn't have to walk. He then followed his boss with Lyly.

The only ones left were Ally and Clay. They really needed to get some new bandages and probably a couple blood transfusions.

"How are you feeling?" Clay asked suddenly.

"Achy. Hungry." Ally admitted.

"No, about all this. I feel like it was only yesterday that we were at the orphanage, no excitement, predictable and mundane."

Ally didn't answer for a minute, thinking. She stepped forward and pulled Clay close in a hug. It felt like she was going to break his ribs, but he didn't pull away. He needed this, and he knew that she did too.

Clay hugged his sister, patting her on the back. "Yeah, me too but at least we have each other, right?"

"Mmm." Ally mumbled.

"What?"

"That was corny."

"No, it wasn't!"

"Yes, it was. Corny Clay." Ally giggled.

Clay couldn't help but start to laugh too. They were going to be alright. He now knew that he was strong enough to protect her. Not that she needed it, she was just as strong.

"From heaven to hell, I'll stick by you Al," Clay smiled, and together they walked after the rest of the group, ready to face the world.

ABIGAIL C. HILL has had an unlimited imagination, passion for writing and a gift of creating new worlds and characters at a young age. She created the concept & began developing the trilogy *The Siberia Path* while in high school. Following the completion of *The Siberia Path* series, she has plans for other stories involving the same unique universe and characters.

Ms. Hill lives in Ohio with her family and 2 dogs, Wanda and Xander.

For more information, go to
www.achillpublishing.com.